SUNSHINE EVERY MORNING

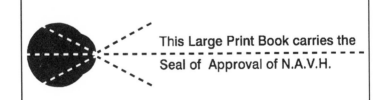

This Large Print Book carries the
Seal of Approval of N.A.V.H.

SUNSHINE EVERY MORNING

DOROTHY GARLOCK
WRITING AS DOROTHY GLENN

THORNDIKE PRESS

An imprint of Thomson Gale, a part of The Thomson Corporation

Detroit • New York • San Francisco • New Haven, Conn. • Waterville, Maine • London

LIBRARY OF CONGRESS CATALOGING-IN-PUBLICATION DATA

Glenn, Dorothy.
  Sunshine every morning / by Dorothy Glenn.
    p. cm. — (Thorndike Press large print famous authors)
  ISBN-13: 978-0-7862-9275-2 (hardcover : alk. paper)
  ISBN-10: 0-7862-9275-X (hardcover : alk. paper)
  1. Large type books. I. Title.
  PS3557.A71645S86 2007
  813'.54—dc22
                                     2006039630

Published in 2007 by arrangement with Spencerhill Associates Ltd.

Printed in the United States of America on permanent paper
10 9 8 7 6 5 4 3 2 1

This book is dedicated with love
and gratitude to a special friend,

GLENN HOSTETTER

CHAPTER ONE

"You can't mean that!"

"I do mean it, Gaye," Alberta said firmly. "I'm asking you to help me save a life."

"You're callous and heartless to even suggest such a thing! It's . . . primitive!"

"I'm sorry you feel that way about it. The baby desperately needs your milk, or I wouldn't ask this of you."

"Would you have asked if . . . ?" Gaye was unable to get the rest of the sentence out past the lump in her throat.

"If your baby had lived? Yes. And you may have felt differently, too," Alberta said matter-of-factly, her hands buried in the pockets of her white coat, her fists clenched helplessly. "There was absolutely nothing we could do to save your baby, Gaye. Some infants born with an open spine can be saved. It wasn't possible with yours." Her voice softened as she looked into her sister's pain-filled eyes.

"I know, Alberta. You told me that, but it's such a kick in the teeth." Slender fingers worked at the edge of the sheet covering her. "It's so unfair — I took good care of myself. I did everything I was supposed to do."

"It wasn't your fault," Alberta said soothingly. "These things happen sometimes, and there are no reasonable explanations."

"I thought something wonderful was going to happen to make up for the miserable time I spent with Dennis." Gaye pushed the heavy brown hair back from her face and looked up at her sister with brown eyes full of misery. "You're strong, Alberta. You've always known that you wanted to be a doctor, and you set about to make it happen. All I ever wanted out of life was a loving husband and children. My husband turned out to be a louse who married me for my inheritance, and my baby couldn't live outside my body."

"It's taken me years to get my life in order after Marshall died. Give yourself time, honey. I'm ten years older than you, and I've learned that healing takes time." Alberta looked affectionately at her younger sister, who looked nearer age eighteen than twenty-eight.

There was little resemblance between the

two women. Alberta was tall and broad shouldered, with a sturdy body and large hands and feet. Her square face was framed with dark hair cut bluntly and styled so that it required little care. Gaye, on the other hand, was the epitome of a feminine woman.

"Please think about it, Gaye."

Gaye moved the rich dark-brown hair from her neck with a nervous gesture and gazed up at her sister with soft brown eyes. Even now, with their curly gold-tipped lashes tear-glazed, they were beautiful.

"Why can't the mother nurse it?" The skin on her face was matte white and stretched over a perfect oval frame. Her mouth was full, with a natural tilt to its corners. There was nothing flamboyant about Gaye Meiners. She was simply quietly beautiful.

"The mother is a child herself, just a teenager. Her own mother came and took her away less than twelve hours after the child was born."

"They don't want it?"

"They don't want anything to do with it. But it hasn't been abandoned. Its grandfather is very interested in its welfare. It's a long story, and I'd rather not go into it now. I'm not interested in the mother, father, or the grandparents. The baby is my concern. I've got to find a formula that agrees with the child or it'll die."

"Why don't you fly it to the Mayo Clinic?" Gaye blew her nose on a tissue and tossed it in the wastebasket.

"That's what I'll have to do if I can't find a supply of mother's milk that agrees with him. We have a small supply on hand, but there's a desperately ill baby who needs it. This hospital isn't large compared to some, little sister, but we do our best for our patients."

"I know that. I didn't even consider going anywhere else when my baby was due. Oh, Alberta! How long will it take before this heavy lump leaves my heart?"

"It will never leave completely, honey. A part of you is gone forever. It's something that'll stay with you for the rest of your life, and you have to learn to live with it. What I'm asking you to do now is help me save this baby. It's a tiny, helpless little human being that deserves a chance to live."

"Do I have the milk?"

"Yes, but it remains to be seen if it's the right milk for the child. If it isn't, I'll have to risk transporting the baby elsewhere."

"Is it the baby I've heard crying so much?"

"No. This little fellow is too weak to cry very loud. We're feeding him intravenously now." Alberta looked at Gaye. "Shall I bring the baby?" she asked hopefully.

Gaye nodded her head only slightly, and her sister quickly left the room.

What am I doing? Gaye thought wildly. I was going to breast-feed *my* baby. Oh, Mary Ann! I'd have loved you with all my heart and soul! I'd have built my life around you. Tears streamed from her eyes and ran into the hair at her temples. It seemed the well of tears would never run dry. They had run almost constantly during the last twenty-four hours, since Alberta came with the news her child had died. She wiped them on the edge of the sheet covering her and turned on her side so she could watch the doorway.

The small, plump nurse who'd been assigned to her came into the room. "Doctor says I'm to get you ready to nurse. You'll have to wear a mask, too. This little'n has had a bad time ever since he saw the light of day."

"The baby's a boy?" Gaye asked while the nurse fussed over her with disinfectant.

"He's the cutest little black-haired fellow you ever saw. I don't know how that girl could have gone off and left him. I'll swear to goodness. What's the world coming to?"

"Alberta said she's only a child herself."

"Humph!" The old-fashioned snort sounded strange coming from the young nurse. "Child, my foot! She's old enough to know what made the baby in the first place. She should have been forced to take care of her child — at least feed it until the doctor could figure out a formula that'll stay put on his stomach. Between you and me, the mother has less sense than the girl!"

"My milk may not be right for it." It was a strain for Gaye to even talk about it.

"The doctor thinks it's worth a try."

The nurse was bending over her, so Gaye failed to see Alberta come into the room with the tiny bundle in her arms until she was beside the bed. The nurse quickly slipped a gauze mask over Gaye's mouth and nose and stepped back.

"What do I do?" The words came hesitantly. Her heart was beating like a trip-hammer.

"I'll show you." Alberta's voice was muffled behind the mask that covered her mouth. She placed the baby in the crook of Gaye's arm. Gaye tried not to look at it. Instead, she kept her eyes on her sister's face. The small bundle felt warm and cozy against her side. This is the way I'd have held Mary Ann, she thought, and her eyes misted.

"We'll put a bit of milk in his mouth so he can get a taste of it." Alberta's fingers worked at Gaye's breast, and the milk began to flow. "C'mon, little fellow," she urged and shook the small head to awaken him. "C'mon and give it a try."

Gaye could feel the small mouth on her nipple, but there was no movement. He seemed so lifeless. She looked down. His little face was pinched, and small veins throbbed just beneath the delicate skin on his temples. He was so thin! Gaye's arm tightened around the small bundle of life, and it suddenly became the most important thing in the world to her that this tiny mite get sustenance from her breast.

"Let me," she whispered. Instinctively her fingers slid over her breast, and she moved the nipple against the still lips. She rubbed it back and forth desperately until the baby stirred and a frown wrinkled its little face. A tiny tongue came out and licked the drop of milk from its lips. Then its mouth surrounded the nipple, and after several seconds, Gaye felt the sharp tingling pain that lasted for only a short while. "That's the way to do it, little man," she breathed. "Keep going. You're doing fine." She raised shining eyes to her sister. "He's sucking!"

"Thank God! I was afraid he was too weak."

Gaye held the infant close. For the first time since Alberta had come with the news that her own baby had died, she felt an instant of peace. Her sister and the nurse stood smiling down on her as if she had created a minor miracle.

"How old is he?" Gaye watched the baby's face grow pink from the effort to draw the milk.

"Five days. He's lost almost a pound of weight. He didn't have a lot to start with."

"Dr. Wright!" A masculine voice, heavy with concern, resounded down the hall.

"Oh, for heaven's sake!" Alberta turned from the bed. "It's Jim." Heavy footsteps came rapidly down the corridor. "He's like a bull in a china cabinet," she said irritably and moved toward the doorway. It was filled by the body of a big man before she could reach it.

"The crib's empty! Where's the boy?" The voice, loud and deep, filled the room.

"Don't shout, Jim! The boy's being fed." Alberta put her hand on the man's chest and backed him out of the doorway and into the hall. "I had an idea. Let's go have coffee and I'll tell you about it."

In the few seconds the man stood in the

doorway, Gaye's eyes took in everything about him, and he frightened her as no other man had ever done. Not only was he big, but his hair was jet black, thick and wild. His brows were as dark as his hair and were drawn together over a large, bony nose. He had high cheekbones, and his flat cheeks were creased in deep grooves on each side of his wide, full-lipped mouth. It was a rough-hewn face with a jaw set at an almost brutal angle. His large, slanting eyes gleamed darkly from between a brush of thick lashes. They darted around the room, passed over her and away. Thank goodness! she thought.

The man had to be a lumberjack, a stevedore, or a steelworker. His jeans were tucked into the tops of calf-high boots, and a faded flannel shirt was tucked into the low waistband of his jeans, the sleeves rolled up to the elbows. Dark hair covered muscular forearms. Gaye could still see him in her mind's eye as her sister's voice retreated down the hallway.

"Who was that?" Gaye spoke softly through the gauze mask, as if she was afraid the man would hear her.

"Jim Trumbull." The nurse giggled. "The name fits the man, doesn't it?" She pulled a chair up to the bed and sat down. "He's a

15

real fistful of man! But nice." She bent over and looked into the baby's face. "We'll let him have a little more and then I'll burp him."

"But who is he?" Gaye asked again.

"The little fellow's grandpa, and he's taking the job seriously. He's here at least three times a day. I think he's sweet, even if he does scare the aides half to death. How he could have got mixed up with that cold-hearted woman who breezed in here and whisked their daughter away is beyond me." She stopped abruptly. Color rose in her cheeks. "Oops! Old big-mouth shouldn't have said that. Doctor hates gossip." She threw a towel up and over her shoulder. "Let me have him. Oh, little boy, I hope you don't throw it all up." She held the baby to her shoulder and patted his back gently.

Gaye looked down at her breast with its enlarged wet nipple before she covered it with the sterile cloth. It hadn't been the traumatic experience she'd expected it to be. It had seemed natural to feed this baby that wasn't her own flesh and blood. She watched the nurse handle it confidently, her hands in just the right places on the tiny body to give it support.

"Do you have children?"

"I'm not married. I want a family someday. "There . . . he let out a little air, and not too much came up with it. Just a little more, baby, and you can eat again."

Later that evening, Gaye was sitting in a chair beside the bed when her sister came into the room. Alberta was dressed to leave the hospital.

"Gaye, you've given the Trumbull baby a new lease on life. We'd like to have you feed him every three hours during the night and tomorrow, then we'll see about putting him on a four-hour schedule."

Gaye's brown eyes were full of misery when she looked at her sister, the doctor. "Alberta . . . can't you pump the milk and feed him with a bottle?"

"We could do that. But we feel the little fellow needs to be held and cuddled. You see, all he'd known was the warm cavern of his mother's body, and now, suddenly, he's been thrust out into the world with nothing to cling to. I've always believed that the secure feeling a mother gives a child while it's nursing is a large part of that child's sense of belonging to a family unit." Alberta sat down on the edge of the bed.

"I'm not his mother! You'll have to find someone else. I'm leaving here tomorrow or the next day. I've got to make burial arrangements for my own baby." Gaye's fingers twisted around each other.

"Arrangements are made, honey. I arranged for a graveside service tomorrow afternoon."

Gaye looked stricken. "Thank you," she murmured. After a hesitation, she said, "I'm going."

"Of course you are. I'll be with you every minute. Then you're coming back here for a few more days."

"There'll be no need for me to come back here. I'll go to your house for a while — that is, if I've not worn out my welcome."

"Don't be foolish. You know you have a home with us for as long as you want. You'd be fine with us. My housekeeper would take good care of you. But I'm asking you to come back here and help me until I can get something worked out for the Trumbull baby."

"He's not my responsibility!"

"I know. He's mine. Stay and help me with him. What's a few days out of your life when it could make all the difference in his?"

"You're not being fair!"

"I know." Alberta's face was set with determination. "When it comes to the life of one of my patients, I'll fight with any means I have. Stay, Gaye. Stay and help me give this infant a start, and I promise you I'll do everything in my power to find a formula he can thrive on."

"Why is mother's milk so important to this baby?"

"I'll try and explain without getting too technical." Alberta paced the room, the heels of her dress shoes making faint clicking sounds on the tile floor. "Several antibiotic properties present in human milk help protect the infant against many infectious and noninfectious disorders. Colostrum contains a large number of leukocytes, which kill bacteria and fungi. Also, there's lactoferrin, an anti-infective protein that helps retard the growth of bacteria by binding available iron." She paused and looked at her sister's wide-eyed, attentive face. "Is this too much for you to absorb all at once?"

"I'm familiar with some of the terms. I got material on the subject from the La Leche League and studied it."

"I know you did." Alberta saw the bleak look come into Gaye's eyes and wondered for the hundredth time if she was doing the right thing in forcing her to care for another infant, even though it was beneficial to both. Professional concern for her two patients took over, and she began to talk. "Breast milk is the correct temperature, and it provides essential nutrients and contains the correct composition of immunological properties that can't be synthesized or added to commercial formulas. But those are only some of the advantages breast-feeding has over formula feeding."

"Enough! You sound as though you're teaching a class. I'll stay a few days, and then you'll have to give me something to dry up my breasts. You know I wouldn't be able to live with myself if I didn't stay and the baby . . . didn't make it."

"Thanks." Alberta gave a big sigh of relief. "Have you made plans for what you'll do when you're well again?"

"Not really. I'd planned to buy a house near here and devote my life to raising my child. Now I think I'll still buy a house, but I've got to fill my days somehow. I don't want to go back to teaching. My inheritance is still intact, and I can live off the interest if I'm careful. At least I was smart enough not to let Dennis get his hands on that. Why I ever did anything as stupid as to marry that creep is beyond me."

"You were lonely — he was charming. It happens all the time," Alberta said flatly. "You were buried in that little town, first with Mom's illness, then Dad's. You were an easy mark, honey, for an opportunist like

20

Dennis. But that's all water under the bridge. You'll know better next time."

"There won't be a next time!" Gaye said with emphasis. "Any fool that would let herself be wooed and wed in less than a month should be kept in a cage."

"Don't be so hard on yourself. You're a natural mother and homemaker, and your instincts were reaching out. It just happened that Dennis came into your life when you were at your most vulnerable. Give yourself credit for seeing him for what he was and taking the steps to get rid of him."

"I knew within the first month it wouldn't work. Soon after that I knew I was pregnant."

A girl carrying a tray hesitated in the doorway until Alberta motioned her into the room. "I've been invited to dinner with a very interesting, but unusual man," she said after the girl had placed the tray on the bedside table and left the room. Alberta lifted the cover and sniffed. "Hummm . . . chicken. Looks good and smells better. See that you eat it all. One advantage of a small-town hospital is the home-cooked meals. That and the prices they charge," she added dryly. She bent and placed a kiss on her sister's forehead. "The night nurse knows where to reach me if there's a need. See you in the morning. Okay?"

"Okay." Gaye grabbed her hand. "Thanks for loving me." Moisture filled the big brown eyes. "I don't know what I'd have done without you." She smiled through her tears. "How's that for an old cliché? It may be overused, but in this case, true."

"It isn't hard to love you, little sister." Alberta squeezed the slender hand she held in her large one. Her features softened, and her professional expression dropped from her face like a cloak. "This is the beginning of a new life for you, honey. From now on it'll be downhill all the way," she promised.

Gaye was exhausted when she returned from the graveside service the following afternoon. Gratefully, she crawled into the high hospital bed and stared at the white ceiling. There'd been five people at the service besides the minister: Alberta; her two teenage children, Brett and Joy; and Candy, the nurse from the maternity ward. It was nice of Candy to come, Gaye thought wearily and closed her eyes. The beginning, Alberta said. I suppose if one thing ends, another automatically begins.

The quiet was disrupted by the lusty cries of an infant being carried down the hallway. A nurse came into the room carrying the child.

"My! What a pair of lungs!" she said with exasperation. "I'm sure they can hear him down on the main floor." She handed the sterile cloth to Gaye so she could wash her breast. "Here, here, now . . . ," she crooned to the still-crying infant. "You'll have your dinner in a minute."

Blessed quiet prevailed the instant Gaye put the baby to her breast. The little lips pulled with gusto, and a tiny fist pounded against the white globe. The angry redness gradually left his face and was replaced with a glowing pink as he sucked contentedly.

"We can't believe the change in this child. We scarcely heard him cry above a whimper until today."

Gaye ran her fingertips over the fine hair at the baby's temple. If only you were my little boy, she thought. She wiggled her finger into the tiny fist. He grabbed it with surprising strength.

"Don't give him too much before you burp him," the nurse cautioned. She left the room and quietly closed the door.

Gaye's eyes clung to the child's face. Yesterday his skin had a sallow, yellowish tinge. Today it was a healthy pink. If only I could keep him, she thought and instantly chided herself for the ridiculous notion. It was impossible, of course. People didn't give their babies to strangers. Well, some people did, but it was beyond her comprehension that they could do so. What kind of a girl would go away and leave this precious infant? At that moment, dark midnight-blue eyes looked into hers.

"I know you really can't see me, baby. You're too young to focus your eyes," Gaye said softly. "But if you're thanking me for your dinner, you're welcome." She stroked the satin-soft skin of his cheek with her fingertips. "I think you've had enough for now. Let's get some of that air out of your tummy and make room for more."

She placed the infant on her stomach and patted his back. Soon small puffs of air came from the tiny lips, and Gaye smiled her satisfaction. I must tell Alberta to hurry and find a formula for you, she said silently to the baby. Or I may get to liking you too much.

The next few days marched by rapidly.

It was evening. Gaye sat in a chair beside the window and looked down onto the neatly fenced yards that backed up to the hospital grounds. Women were raking and burning leaves and children played kickball in the street, while husbands and fathers stacked the firewood that would cut the heating bills during the long, cold Kentucky winter.

Family. It was a magical word to Gaye. It meant a kinship group, a clan of close-knit, caring creatures. Alberta and her two children were a family, and she, Gaye, lived on the fringe of it, loved as sister and aunt. Shattered was her dream to be loved as a wife and mother, the nucleus around which a family is formed.

She had to get out of there! She needed to get herself back together and get on with her life. Thoughts swirled around in her head, disconnected, half-formed thoughts. She could go back to teaching . . . join the Peace Corps . . . open a plant shop . . . find a place on the cold, rocky coast of Maine and hibernate!

Gaye sat with her back to the door and hugged the blanket-wrapped baby to her. She brought the tiny fist curled about her finger to her lips and kissed it.

"What does the future hold for you, little man? Will you have someone to love you and teach you to love in return?" she murmured. "Will you be a giver or a taker? Will you grow strong in body and mind, or will you —"

There was no sound to alert her to the

presence that filled the doorway behind her, but she knew it was there and looked quickly over her shoulder. He leaned lazily against the door casing, looking very much the same as he had the other time he appeared there. He was dressed about the same — jeans, denim shirt, sleeves rolled to the elbows, heavy boots. Gaye stared stupidly. He was a dark, wild-looking man with eyes as black as coals and thick black hair that curled and twisted in complete disarray.

He stared. Gaye felt the hot blood stain her cheeks. She pulled her nipple from the baby's mouth and quickly covered her breast. The child let out a loud yell of protest, and she was forced to turn her attention back to him. The small face knotted with anger, and tiny fists flayed the air.

"Shhhh . . ."

"What's the matter? What did you do to him?" The man seemed to have leaped across the room.

"Shhh . . . shhhh . . ." Gaye bent over the baby and patted his bottom, but the cries continued.

"What's the matter with him?" the voice boomed. He hunkered down beside the chair and leaned over to peer into the baby's face. His head was so close to hers, Gaye felt the brush of his hair against her cheek.

"He's hungry."

"He's what?"

"Hungry." Gaye repeated the word more loudly so he could hear over the baby's loud, angry screams.

"Is that all?" Relief tinged with impatience was in his voice. "Then feed him."

She looked into the dark face only inches from her own. The power and strength of it was obvious. It was the expression in his eyes that grabbed at hers and held them. Although they were piercing, inquiring eyes, they were also filled with great pain. She tore her eyes away, unable to bear the close scrutiny of his.

"Feed him," he said again.

Gaye's eyes swung back to his, wide with surprise. "I will . . . later."

"Feed him now. For God's sake, woman! I've seen the female breast before."

"I'm sure you have," she snapped. "But not mine!"

"Let the boy eat. I want to talk to you." He reached over and pulled aside the robe covering her breast.

"Stop that!" Instinctively she held the baby to herself in an attempt to hide her breast from his eyes. The small mouth grasped the nipple, and the crying ceased.

She tugged the end of the blanket up and over her breast and the baby's contented face. Her own face burned with embarrassment, fired by the deep chuckle that came from the man's throat.

"Why are you so embarrassed? Good Lord! I've seen all shapes and sizes of the female breast — white, black, red, yellow, firm, sagging, small and large. Yours are very nice. In fact, they're beautiful. They're performing the function they were created to do, as well as to arouse male sexual desire."

"Please . . . get out of here!" Embarrassment was beginning to choke off her breath.

"No," he said flatly. He moved, still hunkered down, and rested his back against the wall. "I want to talk to you. Alberta tells me you're divorced. No strings."

"She had no right to tell you that."

"Sure she did. She's your doctor and your sister. I want you to come home with me and take care of MacDougle."

"MacDougle?"

"Yeah, MacDougle."

"You didn't name him *that*."

"What's wrong with it? My mother's name is MacDougle."

"That's no reason to burden this child with a horrible name he'll have to live with for the rest of his life," she snapped.

"John MacDougle Trumbull. It's a solid name. It sounds . . . responsible."

"John? That's better. *MacDougle* would be nothing but a handicap to him. Can you imagine starting school and trying to write it? John or Johnny isn't so bad."

"Not John*ny.* John."

"Johnny is a sweet name for a sweet little boy," Gaye said testily.

"Alberta says MacDougle can go home. I've got everything I think he'll need. Will twelve dozen diapers be enough? I won't have him wearing those paper things."

Gaye gritted her teeth. The nerve of the man! "I haven't applied for the position of nursemaid, and I don't care how many diapers you have, Mr. Trumbull."

"Call me Jim. Now look here, Gaye. The boy needs the best I can get for him. I've watched you walk down to the nursery to look at him, and I've passed this door a few times and looked in to see you holding him. You like him. You like him a lot. Don't try and tell me you haven't become attached to him."

"Of course I like him! I'd have to be out of my mind *not* to like him. And . . . you had no right to spy on me!"

"Good Lord!"

"Oh . . ." Gaye suddenly remembered the baby had to be burped. Under cover of the blanket, she pulled the nipple from his mouth and folded the robe over her breast. She lifted him to her shoulder and patted him gently on the back.

"Can I do that? I've yet to hold my grandson." Large hands, with a generous sprinkling of fine black hair on the back, reached for the child. He was so close to her that his chest pressed against her knees. "That battle-ax of a nurse won't let me in the room where they keep him. I have to look at him through the glass, like he was a monkey in a cage at the zoo."

"They can't let just anyone in the nursery."

"I'm not just *anyone.* I'm the boy's grandpa."

"I'm sure you told her that."

"Several times." He was looking at her mouth. His eyes reluctantly moved to the baby lying in her hands. His big hands covered hers beneath the small head and bottom.

"Put one hand to the back of his head and the other one to his back," she warned. "Hold him up against your shoulder and . . . pat gently."

"Lord! He's so little."

"Not really. As newborn babies go, he's about average size. Pat his back. It'll help him to burp."

"I only have two hands. What'll I pat with?"

"You don't have to hold his head while it rests on your shoulder. Turn his face to the side so he can breathe. He won't break, you know."

"Lord!" he said again. "Are you sure? He's no bigger than the speckled pups I have at home."

Gaye surprised herself by smiling into dark eyes that seemed to swallow hers. This gentleness was completely incompatible with his appearance. She felt a thrill so sharp it pierced her very soul at the sight of the huge man, with the smile of pure pleasure on his craggy face, holding the tiny baby with such loving care.

"He's gained six ounces," she said weakly while her stomach churned with an indefinable emotion.

"You don't say!" He grinned proudly.

"I think he's beginning to focus his eyes."

A small puff of air came from the baby's lips. "Was that it? Is that all there is to it?" He held the baby in his two hands while his eyes searched her face. "Does he have to do that every time he has a meal?"

"He swallows air along with the milk. If he doesn't get rid of it, he'll have a tummy-ache."

"Is that right? There's so much I don't know, it scares me silly," he confessed. He looked down at the red little face. The baby yawned, and he chuckled softly.

Gaye choked back the lump that rose in her throat and looked away from him. He was so big, so proud and rugged, yet he was so helpless where the baby was concerned.

"Will you take care of him for me?" The words hung between them, and the intimacy there was, bordered on tangibility.

"Mr. Trumbull, I . . . don't think so. You see, I —" Her large amber-ringed brown eyes looked at him pleadingly, and the tip of her pink tongue came out to lick suddenly dry lips.

"Won't you think about it?"

"Alberta will find someone for you," she said shakily.

"I don't want *someone*. I want you." He placed the baby in her arms. "You and Mac-Dougle seem right for each other. Say you'll do it, Gaye."

"I don't know —" Her voice faltered. She wished he would go away so she could think clearly.

"Then say you'll think about it," he insisted softly.

"All right. I'll . . . think about it."

"Fair enough." He studied the baby's face and touched his cheek gently with a forefinger. "Raising a child is an awesome responsibility, isn't it?"

Gaye nodded her head and blinked back tears that threatened at the corners of her eyes. She wanted to look at him, but some unknown strong force kept her from doing it.

Finally he stood, and for a long moment he looked down at them. "See you later," he said quietly and quickly left the room.

Gaye listened to his footsteps going down the corridor. It was a sad and lonesome sound.

CHAPTER TWO

"I am not. I repeat, I am not going to that man's house as a live-in wet nurse!" Gaye jammed a soft billed cap down over her rich brown hair and picked up her jacket.

Alberta walked beside her down the hospital corridor. "You know you're welcome to come and stay with us for as long as you want. I just don't want you to rush out and buy a house because you think you've got no place to go."

"I'm far too practical for that. I told the real estate agent what I wanted and the amount I could afford to pay for it. She said there were several places in town that would fill the bill. She's taking me out to look at them. *If* I find something and settle here, I'll help out with Johnny until Mr. Trumbull can make other arrangements. That's all I can promise."

"Don't get carried away and forget about the noon feeding."

"I won't." Gaye put on the rust-colored jacket and pulled the belt tightly about her waist. It seemed strange, but nice, to have a waistline once again. "Isn't it rather expensive to have me stay here and occupy a room just to feed Johnny?"

"Jim is picking up the bill. He'll pay as long as you stay here. I wish you'd consider staying on for a while. I'm not sure you're up to taking care of an infant twenty-four hours a day."

"I can't believe I've agreed to do this. Frankly, Alberta, I'm wondering if I haven't slipped a cog or two." Gaye's brown eyes were so wide and innocent, yet they seemed to sparkle with mockery.

"It's about time you did something impulsive for a change." Alberta smiled at her and pushed open the glass door.

"Don't mention that word! The only other impulsive thing I've done was to marry Dennis. I can only hope this won't turn out to be as disastrous. Is that the woman I'm waiting for — the one in the station wagon?"

"That's Karen Johnson, the real estate agent. She's a nice person. You'll like her. Good luck. I'll be anxious to hear about what you find."

Gaye waved and walked down the sidewalk. It was as if she were walking into

35

another life. I should be nervous, she thought. Happy? Scared? Angry? Confused? Buying a house is a big step, and I'm acting as if it's an everyday occurrence.

Karen Johnson was a tall, solidly built woman with iron gray hair, but she was so alive you didn't notice her age. From the oversized dark-rimmed glasses on her high-cheekboned face to her sturdy brown walking shoes, she oozed confidence. Alberta was right. Gaye liked her at once.

"Fall is a beautiful time of year in Kentucky," Karen said and turned the car onto a street lined with maple trees; the tops had turned a burnished gold, evidence of autumn's frost and the waning strength of the sun.

"Autumn is my favorite season," Gaye agreed. "We had beautiful fall weather in Indiana. The street we lived on had maple trees, and the elms grew so tall that in some places the branches meshed with those across the street."

"Didn't they interfere with the utility wires?"

"Our town was laid out with alleys running the length of the blocks. The utility poles were set behind the houses."

"Sounds like my kind of town," Karen said, smiling.

They'd visited several houses before Karen turned to Gaye and offered to point out the sights. "You were here several weeks before you went into the hospital, and I'm sure Alberta showed you around town, but just in case you missed a few attractions I'll point them out. On the right is our new library — it's really the old library with a new addition. Down the street is the Methodist church, and across from that, the telephone company. These places are all within walking distance of the house I'm going to show you next." Karen gave her a sidelong glance and grinned. "I saved my goody for last."

The three houses Gaye had been shown hadn't really impressed her as places she could call home. Two of them had no yards to speak of, and the third had bedrooms so small they seemed more like closets when compared to the bedrooms back home.

Karen turned the car into a long drive and parked beneath a portico. She turned to watch Gaye's reaction.

"I know I shouldn't say anything negative when showing a property, but in this case I'm going to make an exception. The old Lancaster place may be just too big for you. I want you to see it anyhow. I've fond memories of this place. It was built before

World War One. At that time big houses with large rooms and high ceilings were status symbols. It's been in the same family for a number of years. The owner died recently, and the property was inherited by a friend of mine who lives in Florida. Are you interested in seeing the inside?"

"I've lived in a large old house all my life. How many rooms?"

"Four bedrooms and a bath upstairs. A living room, dining room, small glassed-in breakfast room, kitchen and half-bath downstairs. There's a full dry basement under the house and, as you can see from the gabled roof, an attic that's perfect for storage or can be converted into an apartment if you need the extra income."

"No. I wouldn't want that," Gaye said quickly. She opened the car door and got out. "I haven't seen a house with a portico for a long time."

Karen took a ring of keys from her purse and unlocked the side door. "This is a handy entrance and the one most used by the family that lived here."

Gaye was in love with the house from the moment she stepped through the French doors and onto the gleaming hardwood floors. She loved everything about it, from the wide oak woodwork and narrow, deep windows to the solid wood cupboards in the kitchen. She was delighted with the oversized bathroom, its claw-footed bathtub and brass fixtures.

What in the world would she do with all this room? She could make one of the bedrooms into a sewing room, she reasoned, or into a cozy den. The house was only slightly larger than the one in Indiana.

"I'm afraid to ask how much," she said to Karen as they went up the steps to the attic door.

"You may be surprised. Let me show you the attic, and then we'll go back downstairs and talk about it."

The attic was a large, bare room, as Gaye knew it would be. The roof beams and all the studs were exposed, but it was well lit due to the dormer windows.

"A great place for kids to play on a rainy day," Karen remarked and closed the door.

Gaye sat down on the window seat in the living room and looked out onto the broad lawn. The leaves were falling, and pushed by a brisk fall wind, they banked against the row of lilac bushes that lined the drive. She looked back toward the red brick fireplace and the bookshelves built under the small windows on each end of it. She could visualize her two armchairs sitting there on the braided wool rug she had finished last winter. As she sat there a peaceful coming-home feeling settled over her.

"How much?"

"It's slightly more than the top price you gave me." Karen shuffled the papers in her briefcase and drew out a sheet. "But there are no assessments against the property for street and sewer improvements or other hidden costs. If you're interested, we can make the owner an offer. We'll offer the figure you gave me and see what happens."

"Make the offer. How soon will we know if the owner accepts?"

"I'll call her as soon as I get back to the office."

"My furniture is in storage, but I'll have to buy new appliances. I sold mine with the house." Gaye stood. Now that she had a goal, the world looked brighter. "I may have to borrow or rent a few things until my things arrive."

"No problem. I can lend you some essentials, and I'm sure Alberta can. I'll get Bob, my son-in-law, to haul them for you. He has a plumbing business. He'll check the pipes before the water is turned on, and he'll connect the appliances."

"You talk as though I'll be moving in."

"I don't want to give you false hope, but

I'm reasonably sure your offer will be accepted."

Gaye walked around the outside of the house several times. The property took up the whole end of one block. She liked that. She wasn't used to close neighbors. She also liked the shrubs that marked the property line. She got into the car and for the second time that day she said, "I can't believe I'm doing this."

It was straight up noon when she walked into the hospital and took the elevator to the second floor. She saw Jim as soon as she stepped from the elevator. He was standing in the corridor in front of the glass window, looking into the nursery. He looked at her quizzically and came to meet her.

"Where've you been? MacDougle has been crying for ten minutes."

"It won't hurt him to cry a little. It strengthens his lungs. He wasn't due a feeding until now." Gaye waved at the nurse and went on down the hall to her room. She breathed a sigh of relief when Jim didn't follow her. She didn't realize how tired she was until she kicked off her shoes and sank down into the chair beside the window.

John was angry, and he was telling the world about it in the only way he knew. By the time the nurse reached Gaye's room, he'd worked up a full head of steam and was bawling lustily.

Candy gave Gaye the cloth to wipe her breast and then handed her the baby. The wailing protest was cut off as soon as the hungry little lips found her nipple. Candy went to close the door, but Jim's big frame filled it.

"Excuse me," she murmured and slipped past him and into the hall.

Coward, Gaye thought. She felt as if she'd been deserted and left with the enemy. She pulled the towel up to cover her breast and Johnny's face.

Jim closed the door, came into the room, and sat down on the edge of the bed.

"So you're not coming out to my place to take care of MacDougle." It was a flat statement.

"You're right. I'm not. I've told you that repeatedly."

"Why not? I'll pay you a good wage."

"I want to live in my own house. I made an offer on one this morning."

"Here in Madisonville?"

"Uh-huh. Mrs. Johnson called it the old Lancaster place."

"I know the place. It's big and it's old. What do you want with it?"

"It's none of your business, Mr. Trumbull, but I'll tell you anyway. I sold my home in Indiana and I have to invest the money in another home within the year or pay a huge tax. That's one reason. The other is . . . well, I like an older house with a lot of yard space."

There was a curious silence as they looked at each other. Gaye slowly absorbed his height, his wide shoulders, the soft dark open-necked shirt tucked into jeans. He certainly wasn't handsome, she decided. He was too rough-hewn for that. She looked at his hands. They were work-roughened, with square-tipped, clean nails. The sleeves of his shirt were rolled up. She wondered if they came from the wash that way. His forearms were covered with fine dark hair. Suddenly it struck her that this vitally alive, masculine man was a grandfather!

"You're a grandfather!" Gaye said the words aloud before she could hold them back. "You must have married young."

"Young and brainless. If it had been today we'd have just lived together."

"You sound bitter."

"I admit it. My teenage daughter came to me when she was pregnant because she didn't want her friends to know she was stupid enough to get *caught*. And because she was too far along for an abortion. I'll never know who MacDougle's father is, but I sure as hell know who his grandfather is. I'll see to it that he's taught to be responsible for his actions."

"It seems to me you should have instilled that in your daughter," Gaye said coolly.

"Before that girl came to me I'd seen her exactly four times since she was three years old. She lives with her mother in France. She doesn't like my life-style and I don't like hers."

"If she's a minor she shouldn't be allowed to choose her life-style."

"Exactly. Her mother has custody. I support her and I furnished a place for her to wait out her pregnancy. Believe me, she hated every minute of it. That's about the extent of my participation in my daughter's life."

"She may have second thoughts and want her baby."

"She'll have to go through hell to get him! She signed him over to me, and I've filed for adoption. Is there anything else you want to know?"

"I'm sorry. I didn't mean to pry." Gaye lifted the towel and peeked down at Johnny. She smiled at the picture he made — sound asleep and the nipple half out of his mouth. She looked up and met dark, piercing eyes.

"You have a beautiful mouth. You should smile more often."

"I haven't had much to smile about lately," she snapped.

"I know, and I'm sorry."

The softly spoken words coming from this bear of a man and the steady gaze of his intense dark eyes caught her off guard. Her heart stumbled on its regular rhythm. Suddenly she felt weepy, thinking of her own tiny baby, but she realized Johnny had helped ease her pain. Under the cover of the towel, she slipped her breast back into the nursing bra and pulled her shirt together.

"Do you want to burp him?" she asked, wanting to share with Jim the gift of his grandson.

The grin softened the hard contours of his face, and amusement glinted in his dark eyes. "Mrs. What's-her-name would have a screaming fit, but let's give it a go. I'll be glad to get MacDougle home so I can pick him up without some old biddy yelling at me."

"What old biddy?" Gaye's brown eyes held a definite shimmer of defiance when she met his glance. All her defenses were raised. "You mean Alberta or Candy," she accused him.

"I mean the night nurse — the skinny one with the dyed blond hair, frog eyes, and the face that looks like a road map. I think they call her Georgette." Jim squatted down beside her and carefully lifted the baby from her lap. Gaye placed the towel on his shoulder and tried not to giggle at his unkind, but accurate, description of the night nurse.

"You can pat him a little harder than that, but don't knock the breath out of him," she cautioned.

"I like holding him. I don't think I ever held Crissy." He rocked back on his heels as if he was afraid to get to his feet.

Gaye watched the expressions flit across his face. His lips were stretched in a smile, and his eyes gleamed with pure pleasure. She choked back the lump that rose in her throat and turned her eyes away from him, only to have them swing back of their own accord. She was acutely aware of his broad chest and lean body. He radiated more masculinity than any man she'd ever met. And yet he made no attempt to hide his sentimentality. John MacDougle Trumbull would be loved, there was no doubt about it.

"I don't want someone to take care of him

46

who has no interest in him other than as a way to earn money." His words broke into her thoughts.

"You don't need to worry about that. Whoever takes care of him will love Johnny in no time at all." She tried to smile, but her lips felt rubbery. She tried to keep her voice light, but it rasped hoarsely and caught.

His eyes roamed her face. "I'll pay whatever you want." There was a hard edge to his voice that angered her.

"Wages are not the deciding factor, Mr. Trumbull. I'm not what you'd call loaded, but I'm not destitute!"

"Cut the mister, Gaye, and call me Jim." He got to his feet and loomed over her. "What is the deciding factor?" She didn't attempt to look at him. She looked out the window instead. "If it's propriety you're worried about, my aunt lives with me."

"Then let her take care of Johnny."

"She's seventy years old. I wouldn't ask her to take on the responsibility."

"It's your problem, Mr. Trumbull."

The hard-edged line of his jaw and the sudden narrowing of his eyes warned her that he was angry. It stopped her from telling him to butt out of her life and to take his grandson with him. She turned her head deliberately, her hand reaching for the bell to bring the nurse. With a flick of his fingers he moved the cord out of her reach.

"Not yet." The harshness of his voice rasped across her nerves. His next words brought her up and out of her chair. "I made a solemn promise to myself years ago that I'd never marry again. I'll break that promise to get a good mother for Mac-Dougle."

Gaye swallowed hard. She knew her face was aflame. Then pride surfaced. "You think I'm so hard up for a husband that I'd marry to secure a position? Get out of my room. Get out of my life!" She flung the words out desperately. Anger swept through her.

"I'm not insulting you! I find that most women have a price for . . . everything." His voice was dangerously soft.

Gaye tilted her head defiantly, and her angry eyes raked his face. She wished desperately she was anywhere in the world but here, confronting this arrogant man who held his grandson so tenderly and whose harsh words whipped across her pride.

"I'm not *most* women! In twelve short months I've been married, divorced, given birth to a child who . . . who lived only a short time. I sold the only home I've ever known, uprooted myself to come here to Kentucky because my sister is here. I'm trying hard to cope with all these changes in my life, and I can't handle anything else." Tears flooded her eyes, and she hated herself for not being able to hold them back.

"You need me and MacDougle as much as we need you." There was no sympathy in his cold, no-nonsense expression.

"You have a lot of nerve saying that! I don't need you or . . . anyone. I'm buying a house and moving into it. I won't be your live-in wet nurse and that's my final word."

"You're afraid you'll love MacDougle. That's what you can't handle."

Damn him! Could he read her mind? "What in the world is so amazing about that? I admit it. Does that make me a lousy person?"

He bent over her. She could feel his breath on her face, see the stubble on his cheeks, lashes tangled around eyes so black they were mirrors. "Do you think I'd turn my grandson over to a lousy person?"

"Your grandson has upchucked on your shirt. I told you to keep the towel under his face." He was so close to her, she had to sit down to get away from him. "Take him to the nursery."

"And get chewed out for holding him? You'd like that, wouldn't you?" He placed the child in her lap.

"Hand me the towel." She hoped desperately he didn't know how nervous she was. "You've let what he upchucked run down his neck." Her stomach churned with anger and nerves. She shot him a cool look of disapproval.

"Okay. Let's start again." He sat down on the edge of the bed. "I want, more than anything, to have MacDougle with me. I want to watch him grow and get to really know him. But I can wait for that pleasure if I have to. I'd rather know he's being well taken care of by someone who understands and loves him."

"How do you know I love and understand him?" Her retort was quick.

He ignored her question. "I'm willing to let you take him home with you for a while."

"That's big of you!"

"It's a concession I'm willing to make for MacDougle's sake. I've looked forward to having him with me. I've bought furniture and one of those layout things the store recommended."

"The word is *layette*. Perhaps if you'd been as concerned with your own child she'd be here now taking care of hers!" She had wanted to say something to cut him down. Now she regretted the words, but it was too late to recall them. The silence that followed made her more ashamed of those words than any she had uttered in a long while. She couldn't help the wave of apprehension that caused a shiver to travel the length of her spine.

"You don't know a damn thing about it."

She had to apologize. It wasn't her nature to be rude. "You're right, and I apologize."

"Accepted."

He crossed the room to stand before a framed print that hung on the wall. Gaye watched him warily as he slid his hands, palms out, into the back pockets of his jeans. She noticed how the muscles of his back stirred the cloth of his soft flannel shirt. If his size wasn't enough to draw attention to him, certainly that brawny, earthy, untamed look would have been.

He turned. Their eyes caught and held before she lowered hers on the pretext of giving her attention to the baby in her arms. She was aware, however, that his eyes roamed over her — starting at the top of her head and taking in every feature of her face as they moved to her throat and breasts. His eyes lingered there for a long moment before moving back to her face.

"You have the magnificent quality of calmness even when you're angry. You are the personification of motherhood."

Gaye was startled, touched, and then angered by his remark. "Oh, sure!" she quipped. "You'd say that since you want me to be a substitute mother to Johnny."

"MacDougle," he corrected dryly. "Johnny sounds like a prissy sissy."

"Oh, is that right? I suppose you're going to teach him that big boys never cry and that it's sissy to cuddle a doll or a teddy? Do you think playing football or rugby, hunting, trapping and watching Monday Night Football while drinking gallons of beer makes a man?"

"Whoa! What's got you in such a sweat?" He came to stand beside her. She looked up at him. His eyes traveled over her brazenly. "I knew you liked him a lot!" His eyes challenged her to deny it.

"I didn't say I didn't like him," Gaye sputtered. Then, "You . . . irritate the hell out of me!" She cleared her throat and swallowed hard. "You need a few lessons in diplomacy and child rearing."

"I plan to take a course in child rearing." He grinned at the surprised look on her face. "I admit I'm inadequate in that department."

"That's a beginning," she said dryly.

The phone rang. Jim reached across the bed, lifted the receiver and handed it to her.

"Hello."

"This is Karen and I have good news. Your offer has been accepted."

"I'm so glad! When can I move in?"

"Let's give it until the end of the week. I'll have the house thoroughly cleaned, and Bob will check out the plumbing. The house hasn't been lived in for some time, and something may have gone wrong with the pipes. How long before your furniture arrives?"

"I'll call this afternoon and find out."

"I have a few things you can use, if you're sure you want to move in right away. I'm sure Alberta would like for you to stay with her for a while, but of course, that's up to you."

"I think I need the solitude of my own place."

"Okay, then. If you'll be around this afternoon, I'll come over to the hospital with the papers and we can get the ball rolling."

"I'll be here. And, Karen, thanks an awful lot."

"My pleasure. I'll see you later."

Gaye turned back to the large man at her side. "I've bought a house!"

"You've bought a house," he repeated, taking the phone from her hand and pressing the button for the nurse.

"I knew I wanted it the moment I saw it." Her eyes shone up at him, and she couldn't stop smiling.

He pushed himself away from the edge of the bed. It seemed to her he'd hardly moved at all, but there he was, standing beside her. She had to tilt her head back to see his face. He appeared larger, more rugged, almost primitive.

"Are you always so impulsive? You couldn't have spent much time looking over that property."

Gaye's features took on a look of cool hauteur. Her brown eyes lost their softness. They sparkled now from anger. Before she could retort, the door opened and Candy came into the room, her rubber-soled shoes making little squeaky noises on the polished tile. She skirted Jim's tall figure as if she feared he would reach out and grab her.

"The doctor is waiting to see him," she murmured to Gaye.

"What for? Why is the doctor waiting for

him?" Jim's loud voice startled the baby, whose face puckered for an instant.

"Must you be so loud?" Gaye hissed.

"What's wrong with him? Are you keeping something from me?" he demanded in a grating whisper.

"Nothing is the matter with him, Mr. Trumbull. The doctor sees all the babies every afternoon." Candy hurried from the room with the infant, closing the door behind her.

"You keep Candy and the other nurses scared half to death! I'm sure they'll be relieved when Johnny leaves the nursery."

"I don't seem to scare you." There was amusement in his tone.

"You certainly don't," she said with deceptive calm, tucking a long strand of hair behind her ear.

"You're angry again, even if you do act calm and collected."

He was laughing at her, and she refused to answer.

"You're angry because I didn't jump with joy when you announced you made an investment in a property you saw only this morning. It was unwise of you to plunk down your nest egg without making a thorough investigation."

His rational calmness was all the more irritating. It did nothing to douse the blaze of resentment that burned through her, because deep within, she knew he was right.

"You don't know anything about it. Nothing at all! I'll thank you to keep your opinions to yourself." Gaye felt her throat tighten around angry tears.

"Maybe not. But I know quite a bit about you, Gaye Meiners Hutchinson."

"Gaye Meiners. I took my maiden name back."

"Bitter divorce, huh?"

"That, too, doesn't concern you."

He looked at her for a moment, his eyes narrowed, his face thoughtful. He reached out to run a strand of her hair through his fingers. "It's true. I haven't known you long enough to know much about you. But I do know that you're intelligent, loving, and that you were very good at your job. There's nothing flamboyant about you, Gaye. Although you have a capricious personality that shines through . . . occasionally." His dark eyes lit with mischievous delight when hers became stormy.

"I'm boring! That's what you mean." She tried to push his hand away from her hair.

His long fingers curved around her chin, forcing her to look up at him. "Believe me, you're not boring."

"Don't!" She jerked her chin away from his hand and turned her face toward the window. Nervous hands smoothed the hair back from her face, then welded themselves together in her lap.

"This isn't the time to bring up the subject, not with you sitting there ramrod stiff and . . . all sour, but I need to make definite plans for MacDougle."

"Then go away and make them."

"I knew you'd say that." There was a lilt to his husky voice.

He was trying to keep from laughing! Part of her wanted to hit him. The other part wanted him to go away so she could fantasize about ways to torture him. She clamped her teeth together and refused to take up the challenge to exchange barbs with him.

"Are you so ticked off at me you'll cut off MacDougle's food supply?"

Her head jerked around as if it were pulled on invisible strings. "You think of me as a . . . cow!"

"Oh, my God!" He roared with laughter, and Gaye clamped her hands over her ears. She was sure he was being heard in the center of town. "Oh, Gaye, as petite as you are, no one could think of you as a cow! On second thought, maybe a little brown heifer?" His voice teased, but there was unmistakable admiration in his eyes.

"Alberta will have the formula worked out for Johnny in a couple of weeks. After that you're on your own." There was a quiver in her voice in spite of a supreme effort to control it.

"I knew I could count on you." He bent from his great height and placed his lips gently on hers. The pressure of his mouth was warm and firm, and it moved over hers with familiar ease. There was nothing tentative or hesitant about the kiss. He raised his head, his dark eyes searching hers while his fingers held her chin captive. Slowly he winked at her, then gave her chin a shake and walked quickly from the room.

Stunned by his brazen action, Gaye refocused her gaze on the door after he closed it.

"What's the matter with me?" she wailed. "I'm disconnected from my brain! And . . . I'm talking to myself. That should tell me something!"

CHAPTER THREE

It was the morning after Gaye and Johnny had spent their first night in the Lancaster house, which was now the Meiners house. The doorbell rang and then the doorknob rattled before Gaye could get from the kitchen to the door.

"Cripes!" She could see a dusty black pickup truck parked in the drive beneath the portico.

Jim stood on the steps, his sleeves rolled up even though the ground was white with a heavy frost. The wind was blowing his hair, lifting it off his scowling brow.

"I've been to the hospital. I thought you'd leave MacDougle there until I could bring his bed and set it up."

"There was no need for me to leave him there and make two trips to the hospital in the middle of the night. I borrowed a bassinet."

"You could have stayed at the hospital.

You were in an all-fired hurry to move in here," Jim grumbled and walked past her. His boot heels made hollow sounds on the bare floor.

"If you're going to be a grouch, go away," Gaye said to his back.

He stood in the middle of the room and looked around. "What's a bassinet?" he asked, as if it suddenly occurred to him that he didn't know.

"A basket with legs," she said as she passed him. She went through the dining room and into the kitchen, her sneakers enabling her to walk soundlessly. She wore jeans, and a soft blue shirt was tucked neatly into the waistband. "I'm having coffee. Want some?" Without waiting for an answer, she took a plastic foam cup from the package on the counter and poured coffee from the coffee maker. She turned to see him stooping so he could read the thermostat. "Does the temperature suit you?"

"I guess so. Where's MacDougle?"

"Upstairs."

"Alone?"

"No, I left a mad dog up there with him."

He picked up the cup she had left sitting on the counter. "You're very funny this morning, Ms. Meiners."

"I'm glad you think I'm entertaining as

well as productive."

He roamed about the huge kitchen, his dark eyes searching out every detail from the light fixture hanging over the island counter to the red-brick wall where at one time a wood-burning cook stove had sat. He walked leisurely out to the glassed-in breakfast room. The sun was shining on the frosted trees and shrubs, turning them into sparkling showpieces. When he turned, he was smiling.

"I'll have to come by here every morning to get my sunshine."

"I don't have a monopoly on sunshine." Jim continued to smile. His eyes glinted into hers, and her gaze wavered beneath his direct stare. A deep inner restlessness flickered to life in the pit of her stomach. How come I've never noticed his beautiful teeth? she wondered.

"I'm not so sure." The words were so softly spoken, she wasn't sure she had heard them correctly or that she understood them. She'd completely lost the drift of the conversation.

"You seem to have a lot of time away from your job. Don't you keep regular hours?"

He shrugged. "I work when the mood strikes me." He sat the empty cup on the counter, and she wondered how he could

have drunk the coffee when it was so hot —
she was still blowing on hers.

"What's your line of work?"

"I'm a blacksmith."

"A . . . blacksmith?"

"A welder, too. I like working with metal."

"You're really a blacksmith? Such as in
horseshoes?"

"Yeah."

When it became evident he wasn't going
to say any more, she said lamely, "I guess
this *is* the horse-racing state."

"Are you going to show me the rest of the
house?"

"Be my guest. But don't wake Johnny."

"I'll bring his bed in and set it up."

"There's no need. He won't outgrow the
bassinet for a month or longer."

"Which room is his?" He stood with his
foot on the bottom stair.

"I plan to keep him in my room for the
short time he'll be here."

Gaye led the way up the stairs. All her
nerve endings tingled under the scrutiny of
the dark eyes behind her. Why hadn't she
brought Johnny downstairs? She dreaded
taking Jim into the intimacy of her bedroom.
A shiver of pure physical awareness chased
down her spine. She had an incredible urge
to turn and run out of the house. They

reached the door of her room, and she turned to look into eyes lit with laughter. How, she asked herself, could I have allowed myself to be drawn into this bizarre situation?

His fingers closed over her forearm, and he smiled into her eyes as if it was the norm for the two of them to be standing at her bedroom door. Gaye studied his face, weighing her instinct to trust him against experiences of a past that had almost destroyed her. She waited while he studied her in turn. She didn't really know him, didn't know what to do with him. She wanted him to go, yet she desperately wanted him to stay. A sense of a powerful connection pulsed between them. At the moment it was a quiet, yet profound feeling, but it jolted her into reality. She shrugged his hand from her arm.

"What are you afraid of? I haven't raped a woman for several days."

"Now, you're being funny, Mr. Trumbull." She was shaken and a little out of breath. Where was her painfully acquired self-control?

"Call me Mr. Trumbull again and I'll pinch your cute little tush." He followed her into the room, and his amused eyes went to the king-sized bed and back to Gaye.

Her eyes lost themselves in the twinkling depths of his, and the stiffness left her body. She was conscious of nothing except a warmth and completeness that were new to her. She smiled, and her eyes sparkled mischievously as she succumbed to his charm.

"That's better." His voice was surprisingly soft. "You don't have to be on guard with me. If I kiss you again, I'll give you at least a two-second notice. You'll have a chance to slap my face and shout, 'Unhand me, you cad!' " His lips curled in his best imitation of a villainous leer.

"You may be able to carry it off, even without a handlebar mustache and high silk hat." She couldn't hold back the bubble of laughter.

"I carry them as standard gear. Keep 'em in my truck."

Gaye stood back and watched as he bent over the basket that held his grandson. He had powerful shoulders and arms. She could see him as a blacksmith, stripped to the waist, muscular arms and chest glistening with perspiration as he pounded the red-hot iron. "Under the spreading chestnut tree the village smithy stands . . ." She wondered if Longfellow had such a man as Jim in mind when he wrote the poem. She quietly left the room.

"Come hold the door open for me," Jim said when he came downstairs and found her standing in the bay window. "I'll bring in MacDougle's bed and a few other things I picked up. Seems like all he's got is diapers and things to sleep in. You'll have to help me shop for pants and shirts."

"Pants and shirts?" Gaye followed him to the door. "I don't think you've heard a word I said."

"Yes, I did. You said something about a mustache and a high silk hat." He quirked his brows and grinned.

Oh, God! she thought. His eyes are beautiful, too. "I mean before that." She stood shivering in the open doorway. Jim lifted a box from the truck bed and brought it into the house.

"Something about not having a monopoly on sunshine?"

"Oh, for heaven's sake, Jim! Trying to reason with you is like butting my head against a stone wall. I said Johnny can use the bassinet for as long as he's here."

"Oh, yeah. You did say that." He paused beside her on his way back to the truck. His knuckles caressed her cheek. "He's got a bed. He doesn't have to sleep in a laundry basket. Stop buckin', babe. You don't stand

65

a chance against me and MacDougle."

A few hours later, a bed large enough for a five-year-old stood at one end of the small room next to Gaye's. A blue six-drawer double chest, a different nursery rhyme character painted on each drawer, took up the length of one wall. There were a padded chest full of toys, a rocking horse, a rocking chair, and boxes of clothing and bedding yet to be put away.

"Where shall I put this stuff?" Jim was on his knees, pulling blue blankets out of a box and stacking them on the floor.

"Not on the floor, Jim. Oh, Lordy! Johnny won't be using some of these things for a year. Whatever possessed you to buy them? Three, maybe four blankets is all he'll use. They're not throwaway, you know. I've got a washer and dryer downstairs, and I wash his things every day."

"Okay." He put the blankets back in the box. "I'll stack the boxes in the closet, just in case."

"In case of what, for chrissake? In case we have a blizzard and the furnace goes off, or in case we enter the ice age?"

He stacked the boxes neatly in the back of the closet and closed the door. He leaned against it and looked about the room. Gaye could almost see thoughts forming in his mind and raised her hand, palm toward him.

"Enough. This is absolutely all he needs."

"The room needs a carpet, a curtain and some pictures on the wall." He spun on his heel. "I'll be right back."

Gaye raced after him and caught him at the door. "Don't you dare buy carpet for my floor!" She grasped his arm. "I won't have it. I hate wall-to-wall carpet."

"But something should be on the floor," he protested.

"Why?"

"Why? Well, because . . . good God, Gaye! You're not going to let him play on that cold floor?"

"Of course not! You have the craziest ideas. He's just a little baby. He won't be playing on the floor for months."

"How about a thick, fluffy rug?"

"Oh, my aching back!" Gaye flung up her hands. "I give up! Do as you please, but I won't have any nail holes in my hardwood floor."

"Okay." He grinned and went out the door.

Gaye watched until the truck was out of sight, then went slowly up the stairs. She was worn out from pitting her will against the iron will of this wild, forceful man. It was like swimming upstream against a strong current. Johnny began to cry, and she looked at her watch. Noon? Already?

She carried the rocking chair downstairs to the empty breakfast room. She was out of breath and weak by the time she returned to climb the stairs and leaned against the newel post to catch her breath. You're making a mistake, her mind screamed. You're getting in deeper and deeper. Use some common sense and tell him to get the hell out of here and take his grandson before you find yourself tangled in a web you couldn't get out of if you wanted to. All you have to do is stay firm. You did it once with Dennis. Do it again. Later, she told herself. Later, when Johnny is on formula.

She let down the side of the bed and changed the baby's diaper. He looked so tiny in the big bed. She picked him up and snuggled him against her. It was comforting to hold him. Oh, baby, I mustn't love you too much, she thought.

"You poor baby," she crooned. "You've really got your work cut out for you if you're going to live with your grandfather. You won't be able to call your soul your own."

She sat in the sunny breakfast room, nursed the baby, and watched the birds gather for their annual trip south. Hundreds of blackbirds swarmed to feed on the grass that had been allowed to go to seed. Johnny went to sleep, and she buttoned her shirt. It was peaceful and satisfying to sit there and hold him. Her fingers smoothed the fine dark hair back from his forehead, and she gently touched his cheeks with her fingertips. She examined his hands. They were broad and blunt, like Jim's, she thought idly.

The birds rose and flew like a dark cloud when the pickup drove up the drive. Gaye heard the motor cut off and the door slam. The side door opened and she heard the unmistakable noise of something being slid across the floor. She automatically closed her eyes. She was afraid to guess what he was bringing in.

Jim made several trips to the room upstairs. The thump of his boot heels on the bare wood echoed throughout the house. I'll have to get a tread on the stairs, Gaye thought, or else insist he take off his boots as a visitation requirement.

She shuddered when she heard a pounding coming from upstairs. I won't be upset, she told herself. I won't be upset.

The tinkling sound of a music box reached her. "Gaye! C'mon up and take a look. Is MacDougle down there?" The voice boomed and echoed in the empty rooms.

Gaye groaned. Where else would he be,

for Pete's sake? When she entered the hall he shouted again.

"Gaye!" He stood at the head of the stairs. He saw her — *clunk, clunk, clunk* and he was beside her. "Here, let me take him. You look worn out."

The baby woke. His little face crumpled, and he gave a scream of fright.

"Oh, Jim! Won't you ever learn to be quiet?"

"We'll have to get something on those steps." He took the child from her arms and added, "I'm sorry. But you said it didn't hurt him to cry a little."

"It doesn't hurt him to cry, but he'll be a nervous wreck from being continually startled out of a sound sleep."

"I guess there's a lot I don't know." He held Johnny in his two hands. He had such a happy look on his craggy face it was impossible for Gaye to be angry with him. "Come see what I found at the furniture store."

Gaye stood in the doorway and surveyed the room, now covered with a soft blue rug that extended to within inches of the oak baseboard. A pull-down shade with large, colorful alphabet blocks printed on it hung at the window. A huge gold-framed picture of a clown hung on the wall above the bed, and in the middle of the room, on a metal frame, a cloth swing swung back and forth. Holding the baby to him with one hand, Jim reached with the other and turned a dial on the frame. The soft music of Brahms's Lullaby filled the room. He grinned. He was like a small boy with a new toy.

"Isn't this the damnedest thing you ever saw? We can put MacDougle in the seat, set the timer, wind up the swing, and let him go. It's all done automatically. The same mechanism propels the swing and plays the music. Let's put him in it and see how he likes it."

Gaye began to laugh. She couldn't help herself. "You really are the limit!"

"Is that good or bad?"

"I'm not sure. Look at this room. Everything in it is big. Big bed! Big chest! Big pictures! Even the rug is big." The quizzical expression on his face told her he didn't understand what she was talking about. His head, with its scramble of black hair, tilted. His huge hand rested snugly against the baby's back. His eyes played with hers and then began to glow devilishly.

"Forget it," Gaye said. "Just forget it. Put Johnny in the swing. He may not like it and you'll have to take it back."

Alberta came by several evenings later. Somehow she managed to take time from her busy schedule to stop by the house every few days to check on Gaye and Johnny. This evening she stopped on her way home from the hospital.

"The change in that baby is nothing short of a miracle. I won't be surprised if he's gained a half a pound since I weighed him last."

Gaye smiled happily. "Aside from feeding him, keeping him dry, and washing clothes, there's not much to do." She sat a tall, frosty drink in front of Alberta and handed her a paper napkin to wrap around it. "When do we start the new formula?"

"In a week or two. At first we'll give it to him once a day and then every other feeding. It will be a gradual changeover."

"I'll be glad when he's settled on the formula. There are times when I feel like a milk cow!" Gaye sat down on a borrowed kitchen chair and waved her sister to the other. "Oh, by the way, thanks for the houseplants."

"It was Brett's idea. He's the one with the green thumb." Alberta took a sip of her drink. "Mmmm, good daiquiri. I'd best not drink it all. I'm driving."

"The agent from the transport company called. The moving van will be here next Friday morning."

"It's too bad it's a school day. Joy and Brett would come help you get things settled in the right places."

"There'll be plenty to do on Saturday. I'll take all the help I can get unpacking dishes, books, bric-a-brac, et cetera. I've lived in this bare house almost a month. I'll be glad to have my familiar things," Gaye said wistfully.

Alberta cast Gaye a wary look. "You're not lifting anything heavier than Johnny, are you?"

"No, Doctor." Gaye gave her sister an affectionate smile. "What am I going to do about Jim and Johnny?"

"What do you want to do with them?"

"I want some space. Jim is here every morning. He can't seem to stay away from that baby. He comes by some evenings, too. Sometimes he brings food from the deli, or he brings groceries. My house has become his home away from home." Gaye closed her eyes briefly, then opened them and looked straight at Alberta. "Jim is ruthless when it comes to getting what he wants. He simply disregards any suggestions I make about getting Johnny situated in his home. He acts as if he'll be staying here from now on. Alberta, I'm not going to let that baby wiggle its way into my heart!"

Alberta was a calm woman with an infectious smile and boundless energy. She rinsed her glass at the kitchen sink and sat it in the dish drainer while trying to control the smile she couldn't resist.

"Let him baby-sit," she said when she turned, her face blank of expression. "When he arrives in the morning, be ready to go out. Take that time to shop. Go to the library or to the hairdresser. Jim is perfectly capable of looking after Johnny for a few hours."

"I hadn't thought of that. I do need to shop. I want to order draperies and look for bedroom curtains. I know what I want; it shouldn't take long to find them." Gaye finished her drink. "I wish you'd talk to him, Alberta. He isn't going to look for someone to take care of Johnny unless he's pushed. I need to have a job outside the home, where I can meet people and make new friends."

"He's dead set on you taking care of him. He told me he'd pay you whatever you earned as a teacher."

"Am I supposed to be so grateful for the job that I fall all over myself?" Gaye asked in brittle tones.

Alberta smiled at her unreasonable anger. "We don't want you to do that. Jim was livid when his daughter and her mother were so callously unconcerned about the baby." She leaned back against the kitchen counter and crossed her arms. "The girl came to him when she was almost five months pregnant. He scarcely knows her. She's totally spoiled and mature far beyond her years." She sighed pityingly. "Why wouldn't she be? Her mother lives in the fast lane, and the girl follows in her wake. She'd probably been having sexual intercourse since she was fourteen or fifteen."

"That doesn't say much for the father. Why does he allow it?"

"There's nothing he can do. He and Marla were married for only a year or two. Her father is a judge, her two brothers own a prestigious law firm. The family inherited money. I know Jim has grieved for his daughter but wisely stays out of her life. He sees in this boy the family he's always wanted."

"Why would a girl from that background marry a blacksmith?"

Alberta laughed. "You can't deny that he's a ruggedly attractive, earthy man. He's enough to turn the head of any young woman, and some not quite so young, I might add."

"Not mine!" Gaye said staunchly. "I've had a taste of being under the thumb of an arrogant, domineering man. I won't get into that predicament again."

"Dennis Hutchinson was a creep, Gaye. But you're being unfair if you compare all men to him. I've known Jim casually for about ten years. He and my husband were friends. After Marshall died, there wasn't really a reason to see much of Jim. During the past few months I've gotten to know him again, and I like him. I admire him, too, even though some people think him a trifle strange."

"Strange? What do you mean?"

"He's unconventional, to say the least. Jim could care less what anyone thinks of him. He lives the way he wants to live — a simple, uncomplicated life. But don't let that fool you. He has several degrees, plus a master's in mining."

"What a waste. He has all that knowledge and is content being a blacksmith."

Alberta shrugged her shoulders. "You have a master's, and you're not moving any mountains." She smiled to take the edge off her words. "Knowledge is something that stays with you whether you use it or not, Gaye."

"That's true. But I intend to use mine. What do you think about a day-care center for pre-schoolers?"

"Is that what you want to do?"

"It's something to think about." Gaye walked to the door with her sister. "I don't want to do anything for a while. I need to get settled in here and get to feeling comfortable with myself before starting a new venture."

"Very wise, little sister. I'll try to stop by tomorrow. If not, I'll give you a call."

"I don't think I've ever told you how proud I am of you, Alberta." There was a husky quiver in Gaye's voice. "I want you to know that I love you and I'm so proud of my sister, the doctor. Mom and Dad were, too."

"C'mon . . . that's nice to hear, but you're going to make me all weepy and I've got to stop by the pharmacy on my way home. Doctors are supposed to be all cold-eyed and businesslike." She kissed Gaye on the cheek. "You're trying to ruin my image," she said accusingly and sniffed dramatically.

It was eight o'clock. Gaye had been up since six. Johnny had been bathed and fed and was asleep in his crib. The dented, dust-covered black truck came up the drive and parked beneath the portico. Gaye stood in the window and watched Jim, bareheaded and coatless as usual, get out of the truck. She opened the door.

"Mornin'."

Jim's dark eyes traveled swiftly over the soft rust-colored slacks and pullover sweater that allowed only a small bit of her white shirt to show at the neck. His eyes lingered on the billed cap in her hand.

"Going out?"

"Yes. I have a few errands to do while you're here. Johnny's asleep."

"I brought doughnuts to go with our coffee." He opened the sack and held it toward her.

"I've had breakfast."

"Chocolate covered. The kind you like."

Gaye avoided his dark probing eyes. Lord, but they were dark and deep. His presence filled the big, bare room with a masculine aura that engulfed her. He raised her chin with his fingers, forcing her to look at the warm skin of his throat, past his smiling mouth and into gleaming eyes that locked with hers. He smelled of clean, sun-dried clothes, after-shave and shampoo. His hair was still wet.

"I've had breakfast," she repeated and was surprised the words came out so easily.

"But not with me. Is the coffee ready?"

"I unplugged the coffee maker. You can make fresh." She moved away from his fingers and picked up her jacket. "I'd better get the show on the road. I've got a thousand and one things to do. Make yourself at home." She slipped out the door.

"Gaye!" Jim called from the steps, and she paused on her way to the carriage house where she kept her car. "What'll I do if he wakes up and cries?"

"Change his diaper and give him a bottle of water. Be sure you warm it."

"When will you be back?"

"I'm not sure. It may be around noon."

"Noon? Can't you take time out for a doughnut before you go?"

"I don't need a doughnut, Jim. I had a bran muffin and cereal. What are you trying to do to me? You've brought hamburgers, pizza, tacos, fried chicken and now doughnuts. In another week I'll be headed for Weight Watchers."

"Good Lord! The world won't come to an end if you gain a pound or two. I suppose you want to look like a string of spaghetti."

"That's better than an . . . apple dumpling."

Jim was still standing on the steps, the wind whipping his unruly hair back from his forehead, when she drove her five-year-old Buick from the garage. She was intensely aware of the dark, penetrating eyes that met hers briefly as she passed. It was a man-to-woman look, with not even a smile to disguise it. She waved and tried to quell the unexpected rush of feeling by concentrating on getting past the truck without hitting it. She reached the end of the drive and turned onto the street fronting the house. Damn him! Why was she thinking he looked lonely and disappointed standing there on her doorstep?

Gaye drove down to the shopping center, convinced that she had to do something quick about getting her life back on an even keel. She hadn't liked being married. It hadn't been the blissful existence she'd read about in novels. It had been . . . degrading! She had expected to make adjustments, but she hadn't expected for her life-style to be completely rearranged to accommodate Dennis's unorthodox one.

She had been reared gently and had had no recent familiarity with serious economic insecurity. Her parents had believed with old-fashioned fervor that the family should be the axis around which their lives revolved. Their marriage had been protected and preserved to provide a nurturing environment for their children.

Dennis believed in none of the things Gaye had been brought up to believe in. It was only after they were married that she discovered his true character. There would be no children, ever! The most important things in his life were money and sex. He constantly accused her of holding back on both of them.

He'd planned a courtship as romantic as any she had ever read about — dinner, moonlight, flowers, whispered words of love. He had scarcely touched her until the ceremony was over and he was sure his name was on her checking account. Then it was sex, not lovemaking, on his mind. Sex, when the mood struck, regardless of time or place. Gaye shivered. She'd never told anyone of the horrors of her wedding night. Thank God that time in her life was behind her. She turned the car into the parking lot at the shopping mall, determined to forget Dennis and, for the moment, Jim and Johnny.

Shopping, to Gaye, was a reassuring activity in the aftermath of the confrontation with Jim. She searched the department store for curtains and found exactly what she wanted. She ordered drapes from the same store and walked leisurely through the mall. She paused before the colorful window of a children's shop. She was unaware that her eyes slid past the frilly little-girls' dresses and on to the display for little boys. In the back of the window on a boy mannequin where soft blue denim overalls with a red bandanna handkerchief stitched to the back pocket. "You'll have to help me shop for pants and shirts," Jim had said. A smile curled her lips, and her legs moved of their own accord into the shop.

From the mall Gaye went to the supermarket. She'd brought a shopping list and pushed her cart down the aisles, stopping for dishwasher powder, all-purpose cleaner and plastic wrap. Absently she checked items from her list as she filled the cart, her mind still on the size six-months overalls she had bought. They'll be too large for him for some time, she mused. Will the blue stain on his diapers? Why had it been impossible for her to resist them?

She went through the checkout procedure, and the boy followed her to the car, pushing the cart that was loaded to the brim with sacks of groceries. She looked at her watch. It was only eleven o'clock. She had time for an early lunch or a trip to the library. Suddenly nothing was more important to her than to get back home. How easily the word "home" had come to her mind.

The mailman was coming down her drive when she turned into it. She waved, and then all thought of mail fled her mind when she realized the truck was no longer parked in the portico.

"Oh, no! He wouldn't!" she gasped aloud. "He wouldn't leave Johnny alone! Oh, my God —"

She braked the car and hurried to the door. It was locked, and her nervous fingers fumbled with the key. When she finally managed to get the door open, she left it ajar and ran through the empty rooms to the stairs. Her heart was pounding so hard, it caused a pain in her chest and a heavy throb in her throat. The house was deathly quiet. Fear moved her up the stairs. She couldn't seem to move her feet fast enough.

The crib was empty! Thank God he hadn't left him here alone! But . . . how dare he take that baby out in that rattletrap of a truck! Another thought, one that chased anger from her mind, hit her with the force of a hurricane. Something had happened and Jim had taken him to the hospital! Oh, Lordy! He may have choked, or stopped breathing. What if Jim fell with him coming

down the stairs? Don't panic, Gaye. Don't
panic.

Chapter Four

Gaye dialed the hospital number with trembling fingers.

"May I speak to Dr. Wright, please? This is her sister, Gaye Meiners."

"Dr. Wright has been delayed at her office. May I have her call you?"

"Yes . . . no! Can you tell me if you've admitted an . . . emergency?"

"I'll transfer you to Emergency."

Gaye repeated the question with sobs shaking her voice.

"Not since four a.m.," came the crisp reply.

"Thank you." Gaye leaned against the kitchen counter. Her knees were weak; she was frightened and exhausted. All she wanted in the world was to see Johnny and to know that he was all right. She dialed the number of her sister's office. "This is Gaye Meiners. May I speak to Dr. Wright?"

"Dr. Wright is with a patient, Ms. Meiners. May I have her call you?"

"Has Mr. Trumbull been in with his grandson?" Gaye held her breath while the receptionist asked the question of someone close by.

"No, he hasn't. Is something wrong, Ms. Meiners?"

"No." Relief forced a nervous laugh. "I was out shopping, and when I came home, Mr. Trumbull and the baby were gone. I'm sure they'll be back soon," she added hastily. "Don't bother Dr. Wright. I'm probably just . . . overreacting."

After she hung up the phone, sobs engulfed her. She had made an utter fool of herself! Johnny wasn't her baby. Jim had every right to take him wherever he wanted. She squeezed her eyes shut, but the tears came through her tight lids in an overwhelming flood, pouring down her cheeks and seeping between fingers she pressed over her face.

The past year had been a nightmare. Everything that could have possibly gone wrong had gone wrong. She had thought she'd marked the year off, sealed it and labeled it over. Each morning since leaving the hospital, she had emerged from her bed, checked her mental condition and assured herself she'd forged a splendid facade of outer serenity. She was pleased with it. She hadn't expected inner serenity. Not yet. That was a gift from heaven. Her security lay in the invincible conviction that God would bestow this gift upon her. Now she wasn't so sure. She feared there was a terrifying darkness deep within her and it would never set her free, never!

Gaye moved through the empty rooms and stood numbly by the window. The house was filled with a thick, eerie silence. Damn Jim Trumbull! He and Alberta had practically forced the baby on her. She sniffed back the tears and prayed the leaden weight in her stomach would dissolve. Maybe she wasn't being quite fair to claim they had *forced* her. She was an adult. She could have said a simple no. But she had assumed the responsibility, knowing that sooner or later it would lead to heartbreak. She hadn't expected it to happen so soon.

She looked at her watch. Ten minutes to twelve. Her breasts were full and aching. She paced and fumed. She'd tell Alberta today that this was *it.* She'd tell Jim to take his grandson and get the hell out of her life. She didn't need this anxiety, heartache and throbbing breasts! Gaye's mind spun in giddy circles and collided head-on with the awful truth.

"I don't want to be alone! I feel so damned lonely!" she wailed. Her distressful cry echoed throughout the empty house.

She leaned her forehead against the window-pane. There were two distinct channels of thought floating around in her mind, fighting for precedence. They zigzagged in and around each other. One was loneliness; the other was the conviction that she had made a dreadful mistake when she consented to take care of a baby temporarily. Now she felt as if everything had stopped but her, and she was whirling around and around in confusion, fear and despair.

The black truck coming up the drive chased all logical thought from her mind. Anger started deep down in the pit of her stomach and surged up. It swelled until she was angrier than she had ever been in her life. Her resentment, prodded by her aching breasts, was very real. At this moment she fervently wished she were uninhibited enough to shout every obscene word she had ever heard.

She hastily wiped the tears from her eyes and wondered vaguely if she looked the way she felt — as though she'd been used to wipe up the street.

Oh, Lordy! she thought. He may not have

Johnny with him. He may have taken him somewhere and left him. He could be coming back to tell me he's made other arrangements!

The truck stopped behind the Buick. Gaye flung open the door. She could hear Johnny's muffled cries as soon as Jim got out of the car. He kicked the door shut and hurried up the steps to the door.

"You imbecile! You . . . fathead! Where in hell have you been with that baby? I've been worried half out of my mind!" Gaye's voice was deep, hoarse, and jerky and didn't at all sound like her own.

Jim came through the door without looking at her. He had a rigid expression on his face, and a muscle jumped nervously in his cheek.

Gaye snatched the baby from his arms, unaware that tears had started again and were running down her cheeks. She went quickly to the kitchen, the only place in the empty downstairs rooms where she could lay the baby down. On the way, she uncovered the red little face, and the baby's gasping, angry screams filled her ears.

"There, there, darling, don't cry. Oh, my goodness! You're wringing wet with sweat. What in the world was he trying to do to you? The idiot has wrapped you in *four* wool blankets! Shhh . . ." She placed the baby on the island counter and quickly peeled the blankets from him. "Oh, baby . . . you're soaking wet! Phew! And not only wet! It's no wonder you're so unhappy. It's all up your back!" She glanced over her shoulder. "Don't just stand there," she snapped. "Get me a wet washcloth, a diaper and a dry gown."

"He's hungry."

"I know he's hungry, dammit! But he can't eat in this mess!" She shouted to be sure she was heard over the baby's angry protests. "Shhh . . . darling. I know you're hot and hungry and wet. You'll be all comfy in a minute." Gaye stood back and peeled off her own sweater. She had forgotten she had it on, and trickles of moisture were sliding down between her breasts.

She had stripped the baby and wiped his little bottom on his wet gown by the time Jim returned. She took the warm wet cloth and finished the sponging, then patted him dry and dressed him, completely ignoring Jim, who stood at her elbow.

"What shall I do with these?" Jim wrapped the soiled diaper and gown in the blankets.

Gaye resisted the temptation to tell him. Instead she said, "Put them in on the washer, then go away." Anger was still in her voice. She wrapped Johnny in a light blanket and went to the rocking chair in the breakfast room. With her back to the kitchen, she unbuttoned her shirt and put him to her breast. His cries ceased the instant his hungry little mouth grasped her nipple, and he began to nurse vigorously.

Gaye pulled the edge of the blanket up and over her breast and the baby's face. She was dead tired, both physically and mentally. Her emotions were so strung out she felt like a limp rag, and her shoulders sagged in spite of her efforts to hold them straight.

"Gaye . . ."

"Go away, Jim. Please give me a few minutes to get myself together." She clenched her jaw as her voice lashed out.

"I'm sorry you were worried."

"Worried? You scared the living hell out of me."

"I took him out to my mother's." He came silently to the side of the chair and hunkered down.

"You could have told me you were going."

"I didn't decide to go until after you left."

"I called the hospital."

"You thought . . . ?"

"And Alberta."

"Oh, God! I'm sorry."

"He was too hot. He could get pneumonia."

"My mother said to wrap him up good and it wouldn't hurt him to take him out."

"Babies have a lot of body heat. Why couldn't your mother come here to see him? He's only seven weeks old, for chrissake."

"He didn't start crying until we were on our way back."

"He was hot, hungry and wet. Didn't you take an extra diaper?"

"I didn't think about it."

Gaye looked into dark, somber eyes, then down to the large brown hand on the arm of the chair. It moved up and down as she rocked, but it grasped the smooth, flat surface tightly, betraying his tension. The deep black eyes never moved from her face. He knelt there, strangely quiet. Gaye felt her pulses warm as she realized their intimate position with the nursing baby between them. He seemed not in the least embarrassed, but the force of her own emotions deepened the color in her cheeks and widened her eyes.

"You have lovely eyes," he murmured.

"Johnny goes on formula in a couple of weeks. We can't go on like this," she blurted. "You've got to find someone to take care of him."

"I thought it was settled that you'd look after him for the time being."

"Can't your mother . . . ?"

"No. That's out of the question. My mother is very ill. That's why I took Mac-Dougle to her."

"I'm sorry. But . . . surely you have someone. You can hire a nurse from the hospital."

"They wouldn't have the personal interest in him that you have. But if I can't persuade you to keep him, I'll have to do that, or place him in a foster home for the time being, because I'm going away for a while."

"How long will you be gone?"

"I'm not sure — two weeks to a month."

There was a comfortable silence as they shared their concern for the small life between them. Jim continued to gaze at her. His hand lifted, and his fingers lightly stroked the smooth flesh of her forearm almost absently.

"Keep him, Gaye. You know him better than anyone. I won't worry about him as long as he's with you."

Her mind responded to the persuasion of his quiet, seductive voice. The nearness of him was something she hadn't anticipated as being disturbing. She could feel every nerve in her body respond to the pleading in his dark eyes.

"Don't do this to me, Jim." She squeezed her eyes tightly shut as tears welled. Her heart swelled, and she struggled to keep the sobs from breaking loose. "If I keep him much longer, I may not be able to give him up."

"You won't have to give him up. Share him with me. You love him already. Don't you feel, just a little, like he's yours? You've nursed him, made it possible for him to grow strong. He needs your care, needs to feel he's loved and wanted."

"It isn't my responsibility to supply that. How can you ask this of me? In a few weeks, months, years, you may marry again and you'll want him with you. Or his mother may come back. I can give him up much more easily now than I'll be able to later on. I've got to get my head screwed back on right, set some goals for myself, get on with my life."

"What kind of goals?"

What did she want? Gaye's brain pounded with a million thoughts. Somewhere deep inside of her a yearning was screaming to be heard. Just for a moment, she speculated on how it would be if Jim were her husband, Johnny their baby, and he was whispering words of love and meaning them. She'd always had the craving for the kind of love and companionship shared by her parents. She realized that was the reason she had been so susceptible to Dennis. She had believed him because she'd wanted to believe him. She'd allowed him to charm her with promises and bits of flattery. Too much had happened to her to allow a man to work his wiles on her again. Besides, was that what she wanted, to be tied heart and soul to a man for the rest of her life, regardless of his feelings for her? She'd realized on her wedding night that she didn't love Dennis. But what if she had loved him? Could she have walked away from the marriage regardless?

"What am I aiming for?" She repeated Jim's question. "I guess I want to be . . . happy."

"What would it take to make you happy?"

"I'd have to give it some thought," she said evasively.

"Do you want to marry again and have a family?"

Gaye was shocked by the intensity of his words as well as by his tone. She turned her gaze away from him, miserably conscious of his eyes on her and the fingers that stroked her arm. It seemed to her that the fine hairs on her skin rose to meet his rough touch.

All the emotional bruising of the day seemed to melt and flow away through the fingertips on her arm.

"I've no desire to marry again," she said tiredly.

"What did that man do to you, Gaye? Did he mistreat you?"

"He didn't beat me, if that's what you mean." Her thoughts whipped back to her wedding day. She hadn't imagined her life would be anything but beautiful from then on. How quickly she had dropped from that blissful cloud to the hard, cold reality of living with a man who used every opportunity to erode her sense of self-worth and who'd used her as an instrument of his lust.

"What happened to your marriage?" she asked shakily.

"Marla and I weren't suited. Our marriage was a mistake."

"So was mine. It's in the past. I don't want to talk or think about it." His fingers were curled around her forearm. She felt the same connecting warmth she had felt once before when he held her arm.

"The court gave me custody of Mac-Dougle, but I'd have a stronger hold on him if he had a mother."

"He's got a mother."

"Crissy gave birth to him, but as you

know, there's more to being a mother than giving birth. I'm thinking of the future. There's always the possibility that Marla and Crissy might decide it would be to their advantage to have custody of him. I want my hold on him to be absolute. That may depend on the type of home I provide for him."

"I can't help you with that."

"You can. You can marry me, and we can make a home for him together." Searing black eyes held hers.

Gaye stared at him, pondering her unease. He was clearly an intelligent man; his eyes absorbed everything they pierced, his mind was quick and alert. He was starkly physical. She couldn't deny that her heart fluttered more quickly in his presence. That's a natural reaction, she reasoned. He is an attractive man, and despite my nightmare of a marriage, I'm not an emotional cripple. Nooo . . . her pride screamed. I won't jump back into what I just crawled out of!

"I won't do that and you know it," she said with cool indifference.

"You could live here with MacDougle. I wouldn't move in."

"That makes absolutely no difference. I won't do it."

"You could do worse." He grinned with a

devastating charm that made his rough features beguiling.

What am I doing here? she thought with a pang of fear. Here I sit, nursing another woman's child, talking to a man I've known less than two months about marriage! If I were smart I'd steer clear of both him and his grandson.

Jim sat down on the floor and leaned back against the wall, his long legs extended and crossed. "You're not very good for my ego." He rubbed his firm chin as if he were in deep contemplation. "I guess I'm getting rusty at this courtin' business."

Gaye smiled, relaxed her guard for a moment, and admitted he was intriguingly attractive. Despite his easy banter, she sensed a tension in him.

"You may be borrowing trouble. Surely the court wouldn't give Mac — give Johnny to your daughter and your wife after they left him in your care."

"Correction. Marla is my *ex-wife.* My God! It's been so long I can't even imagine being married to her," he said bluntly with a grimace. "And I think the appropriate word would be *abandon,* not *leave in my care.* Why would they want him back? Who knows? In the crowd they run with, it may become chic to have an illegitimate child. And there's always the possibility he may inherit. As his guardian, they would have control of the funds until he's of age."

"Will Marla's family try and take him away from you?"

"They may not even know about him. But if they do, I don't think the old man would cause trouble after he knows the facts. I wouldn't trust his sons as far as I could toss a piano."

"Poor little boy. There's no one to love him." Gaye was looking at Jim as she spoke and then realized he might take her words to mean a softening in her refusal to marry him. Her lashes dropped quickly, rich crescents of darkness against her white cheeks. She'd caught something remarkable in the jet black eyes that hadn't been there before. It had been tenderness, but a tenderness edged with pain and anxiety.

Under the cover of the blanket, she shifted the sleeping child and buttoned her shirt. Jim got to his feet and stood waiting until she uncovered the baby's face. He reached for him with confident hands and cradled him in his arm.

Gaye watched him leave the room, and then her glance settled on the dusty boots he'd left beside her chair. She foolishly accepted the fact that she had never felt more natural with a man, more comfortable, more female, more excitingly stimulated. Was she falling a little in love with him, or was she just thirsty for all the wonderful raw and masculine enticement he had to offer?

On Friday morning, Jim arrived at the house with the back of his truck loaded with neatly cut wood for the fireplace. He selected a location several yards from the back door, drove two steel posts into the ground, and stacked the wood between them. Gaye was in the kitchen when she heard the ring of the hammer against steel. She knew better than to protest this generous gift; he would leave the firewood no matter what she said.

For the past several days their relationship had been a comfortable one. Gaye's intense nervousness had begun to dissipate as she realized she was in complete control of her life and that Jim couldn't demand anything from her that she wasn't willing to give. She felt it inevitable that they would eventually come together with a clash of wills, and she accepted this; the growing relationship between them was taking away the fear that she'd be unable to cope with the clash when it came.

Later, she meditatively watched him as he worked tirelessly arranging the furniture the men brought into the house from the moving van. He had told her with quiet concern she was not to lift or move even the smallest box, but was to sit in a chair beside the door and instruct the men where each piece of furniture was to be placed. Things seemed to fall magically into place under her supervision and the muscles of the dark giant of a man.

In less than four hours, the last of the furniture was placed on the rolled-out carpets, the last box in the kitchen for unpacking. The moving men picked up their packing pads, drew up the ramp and closed the yawning end of the truck. Gaye closed the door as they drove away and leaned her back against it.

"I knew my things would fit into this house perfectly. Oh, Jim! This is going to be a cozy home for all its size." Her eyes caught and held his. Then she looked about the room with smiling appreciation. Her braided rug fit into the space before the fireplace, the platform rocker and the reclining chair on each side. The large winged sofa served as a room divider. "I can hardly wait to build a fire in the fireplace."

"Can you wait until after lunch?"

"I'm too excited to eat."

"MacDougle isn't. He wants his vittles."

"That boy would put a piglet to shame! I swear he's got a built-in clock. He gets formula this noon." Gaye flashed Jim a smile. "Bring him down while I warm it. And, Jim, when you change his diaper, don't drop it on the floor like you did the last time. Put it in the bucket and close the lid."

"Do this, do that," he grumbled. His dark eyes were alight with humor, and they held hers for a long moment.

"And when you pin the diaper, put your fingers between Johnny and the cloth so if you're clumsy, you'll only hurt yourself," she added, her eyes riddled with deviltry. She felt a thrill of excitement race through her in that moment that their eyes met. There was a certain knowledge of each other, a rapport.

"Yes, ma'am," he said meekly. "Bossy dame doesn't think I know anything," he grumbled to himself and took the stairs two at a time.

The excitement stayed with Gaye while they unpacked the boxes and placed dishes and utensils in the cabinets. Jim carried out the packing boxes and returned to find her standing in the middle of the kitchen with a shiny copper teakettle in her hand.

"I can't decide whether to sit this on the end of the snack bar or on the table in the breakfast room."

"How about on the stove?"

"Filled with chrysanthemums?"

"Flowers? I thought it was used to boil water."

"It used to be, but I had it stripped and polished. When I found it at a garage sale it was nickel plated and all black on the bottom. I think I'll put it on the table and fill it with yellow chrysanthemums."

"It's dented, and part of the handle is burned off."

"Of course. Otherwise, how would I know it's old?" She reached into a drawer for a pair of scissors.

He caught her wrist in his hand and gently removed the scissors with his other one. "I'll get them. They're those yellow things alongside the carriage house. Right?" His hand slid down her wrist and engulfed hers.

"I can do it." Her eyes were intent on his straight nose, wide-set eyes and square jaw.

"Sure you can. I've got the feeling you can do anything you set your mind to, Mama Bear."

"Mama Bear!" Her eyes twinkled at him through a forest of thick lashes. "No one's ever called me a bear. A mouse, maybe, but not a bear!" She laughed with languid pleasure. It had been a long time since she'd felt entirely unrestricted, so long since she'd been so completely at ease with a man. She reveled in the happiness the day had given her.

"A *little* mama bear?" he said hopefully. He placed the fist that held the scissors on the top of her head and gently brought it even with his shoulder.

"But I don't have my shoes on, and you have on those darned old boots!" she protested.

"Am I going to have to carry the firewood in my stocking feet?" He gently nudged her chin with the hand holding hers.

"Nooo . . . I'll put up with the boots as long as you continue to work," she said with false hauteur.

"The woman is a slave driver," he said as if talking to himself. "Small and pretty as a little brown wren, cuddly as a baby bear, but cunning as a fox and as determined as a beaver."

"Thanks a lot, Grandpa Bear!"

"Grandpa? My God! That's right, isn't it? Oh, well, Grandpa is the king of the jungle, you know." His dark eyes held such a teasing, humorous light that his whole face was transformed into a much younger version of the unsmiling man she had first seen standing in the hospital doorway.

"Nooo . . . I didn't know." Gaye was suddenly breathless. "Then he'd better find his own jungle to roar in."

"He's found it." He bent and kissed her on the nose, as if to punctuate the remark.

Gaye's eyes searched his back as he went to the door. He's excessively tall, she thought. He must be six three or six four. He has extremely broad shoulders for a man with such a trim waistline. I wonder what he does to keep so fit. He's a grandfather! He looks thirty-five, but he's got to be at least forty. Could a man of forty have such a startlingly powerful physique? His movement was so assured, as if he were king of all he surveyed. God help anyone who sought to take something from him!

A spate of nervousness struck Gaye, and she felt almost giddy. She'd acted like a stupid schoolgirl. The thought hit her like a dash of cold water. He had reacted to her teasing as any man would under similar circumstances. She sat the teakettle on the table and hurried up the stairs on the pretext of looking in on Johnny, but — she admitted to herself as she stood before the bathroom mirror — it was really to get her head out of the clouds before she made a fool of herself.

When Gaye came downstairs, Jim was checking the chimney to be sure it was clear of birds' nests and other debris before he built a fire in the fireplace. "I put the flowers in the sink," he said. "Am I invited to stay for dinner?" He lifted a log from the copper boiler. "This thing doesn't hold very much," he muttered.

"No, but you've got to admit it looks nice." Darkness had come swiftly, and Gaye went about the room turning on the lamps. "I like my antiques to be useful. I didn't have a fireplace back home, so I turned the boiler upside down and used it as an end table beside a chair. I think it makes a better wood container. I've got an old bellows and an iron ladle packed away somewhere," she announced proudly. "I'm going to put my coffee grinder in the kitchen, and my little black iron hand pump in the dry sink in the hallway. And . . . of course you can stay for dinner. I couldn't very well throw you out after all the work you've done."

Jim was replacing the screen after adding another log to the blaze on the grate. "Come here and I'll show you how to work the damper so you won't fill the place with smoke."

Gaye moved over beside him. He stepped behind her, and it seemed to her his large body closed around her. She could feel his chin on the top of her head, stirring her hair, and when he reached around her, her shoulder was firmly pressed against his chest. She prayed he didn't know how breathless she was and how fast her pulse was racing.

"This brass lever controls the amount of air that goes up the chimney. Turn it to the left and it closes. See how the smoke is coming out into the room? Turn it to the right and the draft takes the smoke up the chimney." His other hand was firmly attached to her upper arm. He loosened it now, and it played up and down her arm from shoulder to elbow. "Are you paying attention?" His lips were close to her ear. Was that his nose burrowing into her hair?

"Of course I'm paying attention." She tried to move away.

"Lesson isn't over." His hand tightened and pulled her back against him. "If you open the damper too wide, all the heat goes up the chimney. The trick is to find a happy medium. Turn the lever all the way to the right, then back just enough so that the smoke goes up and out. Do you get the picture?"

Gaye knew he was looking at her. His hand had stilled on her arm. "Of course I get the picture. I'm no dummy!"

"What's the difference between a dummy and a doll?" he asked softly. His lips were so close to her ear she could feel the warmth of his breath.

"No difference. They both have a head full of sawdust." Her face was so hot it felt scorched. She edged away from him, and he let her go. "You'll have to excuse me. If I'm going to have a guest for dinner, I'd better get with it."

"Who'll be here besides me?" He was standing with his hands in his back pockets. With his shoulders thrown back, the buttons on his shirt strained to hold it together. Once again he looked like the rough, wild man who had demanded, "Where's the boy? He's not in the crib!" Gaye felt the heat of his slanting dark eyes, but it wasn't fear she felt this time. It was an awareness of herself as a woman. She'd never felt it quite so acutely before.

"No one, unless Alberta or Candy come by."

"Good. Let's hope they visit another time. Do you like spaghetti?"

"Love it."

"Okay!" He grinned. "It'll take about an hour. Get yourself upstairs. Take a bath or something. Rest. You've put in a long day. What does MacDougle get tonight?"

Gaye felt another flash of heat on her face. "Ah . . . not formula."

"Good. That'll keep you out of the kitchen."

"I don't have to be hit over the head to know when I'm not wanted!" She sniffed dramatically.

"How about when you're . . . wanted?"

There was a flash of pain in her eyes before her lids slipped over them like obedient servants. "Then it may be necessary," she murmured and left the room.

CHAPTER FIVE

Gaye took a quick bath. Somehow she couldn't bring herself to linger in the warm suds with Jim in the house. She pulled on a peach-colored velour shirt and pants. It was a well-worn, comfortable outfit. It wouldn't do to wear anything too fancy. Jim might get the idea this was a special occasion. Oh, for goodness' sake! This was a special occasion. It was the first night in her new home with all her familiar things. She brushed her hair with a swift half-angry motion and tried to keep her mind off the big man who had come barnstorming into her life.

She fed the baby and dressed him for bed. This part of her life was very satisfying. She carried him to her bedroom and laid him on the bed, bouncing him gently, smiling at the cooing noises he made.

"My, my! You are growing," she crooned. "You're going to be as big as your grandpa someday." She ran her fingers over the fine dark hair. The baby spit and cooed and tried to catch her fingers. "Oh, darling! I don't know if I could bear to let you go now." She picked up the chubby infant and held him to her shoulder. "You can come downstairs tonight. You don't have to stay up here all by yourself when you're so wide awake."

It was comforting to hold the small, warm body. Gaye held him to her like a shield and went down the stairs and into the quiet living room. She sat down on the couch and placed Johnny on his back on her thighs. She caught his flaying hands in hers and patted them together while his tiny feet beat a tattoo against her stomach. She tuned the sounds coming from the kitchen out of her mind and gave herself up to the enjoyment of playing with the baby.

"You rascal, you! You're going to outgrow this sleeper before I know it." She stroked his cheek with her finger, and the baby tried to catch it in his mouth. Gaye laughed with delight. "Oh, no, you don't! You've had your dinner. You don't get another ounce of milk until midnight, and in a few weeks you're going to have to sleep through the night. The only reason you're getting extra now is because you got off to a bad start."

"He's growing, isn't he?" Jim had come silently into the room from behind her and bent to place his head close to hers.

"Of course. He's . . . perfect!"

"Do you think he'll be big, like me?" He reached over the back of the sofa and tickled the baby's stomach with gentle fingers. This seemed to amuse Johnny, and he kicked his feet and waved his arms.

"You'll have to wait until he's two years old to find out how tall he's going to be. He should be half as tall as he'll be full-grown." Gaye felt awkward and confused with Jim's cheek so close to hers.

"Is that right? Hmmm . . . that means he'll be six feet tall if he's three feet tall at age two. You've got some growing to do, Mac-Dougle."

His other arm reached around Gaye, and he caught the tiny kicking feet in his hands. Gaye was painfully aware of being encased within his arms and that his cheek was firmly pressed to hers. A slow, dangerous fire began to seep upward from her toes, and she strove to maintain her quiet composure.

"He's doing the best he can." She could feel the movement of her jaw against his.

"With your help."

He was turning his lips toward her cheek! "I'd better . . . take him upstairs."

"Why can't he stay down here with us?"

His nose was firmly against the hollow of her cheek. "Am I making you nervous?"

"Nooo . . ." She seemed to have two spare hands she didn't know what to do with.

"Well, you're making me nervous — or something. I've got a powerful urge to kiss you. You smell clean and fresh, not all smelly like a cosmetic counter in a department store."

"I wear unscented cosmetics." She said it defensively. She gazed at the large dark hands holding the baby's feet. The backs and the long fingers were covered with fine black hair. They were so close the knuckles grazed her breast.

"You're a rare treasure." The whispered words came on a sigh. He nestled his cheek closer to hers, tipped his face and blew down her neck. "That isn't what I want to do, but it'll have to do — for now."

"Jim . . ."

"Don't sputter. I want to enjoy this. You're nice to hold. Soft . . . well-rounded —"

"Thanks a lot." She tried for flippancy and failed miserably. "It takes time to get back in shape."

"I like your shape. Are you trying to lose weight?"

"Of course! No woman wants to be . . . soft and well-rounded."

"Why not? What's wrong with soft and well-rounded? I want you to stay the way you are." His hands left the baby's feet, crossed each other and moved to her rib cage. "Why do you want to lose weight? Shall I tell you a secret?" His nose nuzzled the hair back from her ear, and warm lips caressed the lobe. "You look and feel like every sweet dream I've ever had all rolled up in one. No, no . . . don't struggle. I'm not going to rush the fence." His arms loosened, and his hands came up to cup her head. "You are one sweet little thing," he muttered, half to himself.

Gaye quivered at the singing tension between them. Her heart beat wildly and a shudder rippled under her skin as she tried to retain her composure. She slid her hands under the baby and raised him to her shoulder.

"Let me take him." Jim was in front of her. His large hands moved over hers as he lifted Johnny from her arms. Her gaze lifted involuntarily to his. There was a mesmeric fascination in the soft, sweet smile that curved his lips and was reflected in his eyes. Her own eyes mirrored her confusion. His head tilted slightly. "Don't worry about it. It'll all sort out."

Gaye had never felt less articulate in her

life. Jim held Johnny cradled in one arm. He extended a hand to her, and she put one of hers into it. He tugged gently and she was standing beside him. The lamplight shone on the square-jawed, craggy face tilted toward the babe in his arms. He placed a tender kiss on the tiny forehead, and a small light exploded in Gaye's heart. Her gaze slid away, but not before he glimpsed the wretched loneliness in her soft brown eyes.

"Gaye . . ." His arm went around her, and he pulled her close to his side. "You can have more babies. You and I could give John brothers and sisters."

"Nooo . . ."

"You could have my baby, Gaye." The softness of his voice turned her to butter.

She broke away from him and walked rapidly to the kitchen. Doubtless Jim would make beautiful, strong children. She was acutely aware that when he touched her, looked at her, her nerves danced along the entire length of her spine. With her natural nurturing instincts, the offer was tempting. She would love to have another baby — Jim's baby — but she wasn't sure she would survive the explosion of more fragmented dreams.

"Shall I put MacDougle in the laundry

basket?" The voice in the doorway was friendly, but impersonal.

"Sure. Why not?" Gaye washed her hands at the sink in order to give herself time to get her trembling mouth under control. "I'll get it. It's in the hall. You have to admit it's handy, and it isn't a laundry basket. It's a bassinet." Her voice was calm and disguised her nervousness beautifully. It was a small triumph, and she clung to it.

The meal went smoothly enough despite Gaye's initial doubts. Jim seemed to be superbly at ease, making outrageous remarks about how handsome and smart Johnny was and how, of course, he got it all from his grandpa. It was difficult for Gaye to be casual at first. She felt awkward and ill at ease, but her composure was marble firm, and eventually the meal was over and the dishwasher loaded.

"You're a very good cook," she remarked and hung the towel on the rack after wiping the counter.

"I like to cook. Does that surprise you?"

"Well . . . yes."

"I have all sorts of hidden talents. I can sew on a button with the best of them."

"Brag, brag, brag!"

His smile changed to a roguish grin. "I don't claim to be humble."

"That, I believe!" She put her hands beneath the sleeping baby and lifted him to her shoulder. "Your grandpa is a braggart, Johnny. Let's hope you didn't inherit the trait."

Laughing, he went to her. "I'll take him up to bed." His big, warm hands moved over hers, and he took the child from her arms with gentle sweetness. "C'mon. Let's tuck our boy in for the night."

Gaye took a deep breath to steady the tremor that ran through her. You're ruining my nervous system, she admonished silently as she climbed the stairs beside him.

She waited for him in the doorway and watched as he turned his grandson over on his stomach and covered him with the light blanket that lay at the foot of the bed. His fingers stayed for just an instant on the dark head, and then he glanced around the room.

"This is just the type of home I had in mind for him," he said absently.

Gaye's not-quite-steady fingers found the switch beside the door and dimmed the light.

They went silently down the stairs. At the bottom, Jim looked up at them. "I still think we need a tread on those steps. It'll be safer."

His use of the word "we" almost went unnoticed. Gaye shook herself into alertness. "I plan to have them carpeted."

"When?"

"Soon."

"While I'm gone?"

Gaye lifted her shoulders in a shrug and went into the living room. She sat down on the couch and clasped her hands tightly together. Things were getting out of hand. This was her house! He was taking altogether too much interest in it, and she should say so.

"Jim . . ."

"I'll be gone for two or three weeks."

The statement made her draw in her breath. He had told her days ago that he would be away for several weeks. At the time, she had thought she would be relieved to have him out from underfoot for a while. When had things changed? Two or three weeks suddenly seemed like a lifetime. Oh, for goodness' sake! What was the matter with her?

Jim seated himself carefully beside her. She sat hunched over, her hands on her knees. He touched the hair resting on her shoulder, then traced a finger down over her rounded back.

"Sit back and relax. I couldn't get into those rapeproof pants of yours with a can opener."

Her head jerked around to see the mischief dancing in his dark eyes. "You like to shock me!" she accused, but she couldn't keep the smile out of her voice.

His hand at her waist tightened and pulled until her shoulder was firmly wedged beneath his arm and her thigh was alongside his. He rested his head on the back of the couch and stretched his long legs out in front of him.

"Ahhh . . . this is nice." His hand cupped her cheek and forced her head to his shoulder. "Be still," he said when she lifted her head to look at his face. He was watching her from beneath lowered lids, his mouth curved in a satisfied smile. "You're a very restful woman when you let down your guard. Let's just sit here and look at the fire and not borrow trouble. Hummm?"

"You shouldn't . . . I'm not going to . . ."

She could feel his laugh against the breast that was pressed to his chest. "You're not going to . . . what? Let me stay the night?"

"Absolutely not!"

He laughed again. "We're not quite ready for that, but we may be by the time I get back."

"Jim, don't talk like that!" She tried to move away, but his arms closed about her.

"Why not? I want to go to bed with you. I think you want it too."

"You're crude!"

"You said that before. I'm honest. I don't know anything about this courting business, and I'm too old to learn. I don't know anything about hedging and maneuvering and playing games. I want you, and I'll do everything I can to get you. We're comfortable together, we like many of the same things and we have MacDougle."

"You don't know what I like," she said heatedly. "I don't know anything about you at all! I don't know where you live or how you live. I know nothing of your values. You're taking altogether too much for granted."

"Be truthful. Aren't you just a little bit attracted to me?"

Her face turned crimson. "Why . . . you conceited oaf, you —"

"Don't be embarrassed. Answer my question." His fingers tilted her flushed face up to his. "You better answer or I'll have to kiss you to prove it to you. On second thought . . ."

His hand slipped to her throat, then moved to the back of her neck. He kissed her without passion on her soft mouth, almost as if comforting a child.

Gaye pulled away in confusion, dismayed by the shafts of pleasure his lips sent along her spine. He pulled her back to him and claimed her lips again. The pressure of his mouth hardened — seeking, demanding, willing her to recognize her own need. His tongue stroked her lips, and she allowed it to enter her mouth. Her breathing became erratic as a fire of feverish longing ignited within her. Her voice was barely audible. "Jim . . ."

"It's all right, sweetheart . . ." He was kissing her trembling mouth with incredible gentleness. He kissed her eyes, tracing the outline with sensual, delicate caresses. His kisses moved slowly down her cheek to the corner of her mouth, his tongue moist and probing. Her hand had found its way to the back of his neck, and her fingers buried themselves in the unruly dark hair. She was swimming in a haze, aware only that her body was pressed tightly against his, his mouth warm and tantalizing against her skin.

Gaye's breath caught in a sob as she felt his hand slide up under her velour top and his rough palm caress her naked skin. Shock waves of desire she had thought never to feel again hardened her nipples and twisted her belly. The heavy throb within her caused her to open her eyes and look into his. His eyes drank in every detail of her face, from trembling, kiss-swollen lips to the dilated pupils of her velvet-soft eyes.

"It's all right, sweetheart . . ." he said again. His voice was a ragged whisper.

She took a shaky breath, her voice very low. "I suppose you'll say, 'I told you so.'" She pressed her face against his shoulder and closed her eyes tightly against the mocking words that were sure to come.

"Why would I say that? I think you turned the tables on me. You've got this old heart beating like a trip-hammer." His hand began to stroke her hair. "That first night when I saw you sitting in the chair holding MacDougle, it really shook my timber.

"Do you know what I thought? I thought, oh, my God! I've wasted twenty-five years of my life. I could have had a woman like her and MacDougle could be my son, instead of my son once removed. I'd never really thought about motherhood connected with an attractive woman. The women I've known have been sensuous and sexy. You're the softest, sweetest woman I've ever had the privilege to know." He sighed deeply. "Now that I've bared my feelings, are you going to laugh?"

"No! Why would I do that?" She echoed

his words and turned her face into the curve of his neck.

He laughed and hugged her so tightly she thought her ribs would crack. "I'm trying to seduce you, you know."

"Maybe I'm trying to seduce you!" Gaye couldn't believe the words had come out of her mouth.

His laugh was a deafening roar in her ear. "Oh, good Lord! Nothing that good could be happening to me!"

He loosened his grip on her and they sat quietly. His fingers moved on her cheek, her ear. Absently, his other hand spread out across her rib cage. It was as if they had both run a hard race and it was time to relax and get their wind back.

"I'll try to get back in a couple of weeks," he said after a long silence.

"Where are you going?"

"I thought you'd never ask. I was afraid you didn't give a damn." He chuckled. "I'm going to Louisville."

"Louisville? That's not so far away. I thought you were leaving the country."

"Will you miss me?"

She hesitated. "What will you be doing up there?"

"Putting shoes on some of the most expensive feet in the world."

"Horseshoes?"

"No, silly girl. Patent leather pumps!"

"How was I to know? I've never known a blacksmith before."

"I'll have to bring you a copy of my book."

"*Your* book?"

"My book. *The Modern Farrier.*"

"You wrote it?"

"Sure."

"It has your name on it?"

"Uh-huh."

"I'm impressed! I've never known an author, either."

"You're setting all kinds of records this evening."

She became acutely conscious of his fingertips moving across the skin of her rib cage, his thumb snugly beneath her breast. Exasperated with herself, yet enchanted by him she grasped his wrist in an effort to pull his hand from beneath her top.

"Don't, Jim. You mustn't . . ."

"Be still. We're doin' nothing immoral."

"Jim . . . I don't go in for . . ." she paused, swallowing.

"Casual affairs?" Jim interjected with a grin. "Oh, honey — one has only to look at you to know that. I bet you were a virgin when you married."

"What's so funny about that?" she asked,

bristling.

"I'm not laughing. I'm just wishing the hell it had been me. I envy the bastard. Was he gentle with you?" His last words were an urgent whisper against her cheek.

"It's none of your business!" She tried to slide away. His arms stopped her.

"Tell me about your marriage."

"No! I don't want to talk about it."

"Why did you leave him? You did leave him. No man in his right mind would leave you."

"I left him because I was pregnant and I was afraid he'd . . ." She pushed against him. "Please let me go."

"Let me hold you . . . please." His arms fell away from her. "I'll never use my superior strength to force you. Come to me, Gaye. Let me hold you. It'll be comforting to both of us."

For a bewildered moment the old pain and agony came boiling back with such power that she felt as though she was back in the house in Indiana and Dennis was hurling insults at her because she refused to go along with one of his outrageous ideas. There was an odd despair in her face. She closed her eyes, and when she opened them Jim was holding out his arms. She hesitated for an instant, then swayed toward him. He folded her to him with gentle urgency.

"Ahhh . . . babe . . ."

The tenderness in his voice brought a torrent of tears streaming from her eyes. Something burst within her with a rending force, and she clung to him, inundated by an overriding grief. She hid her face in the curve of his neck. His arms were a band of warmth around her. He didn't speak. His silence was a communication of its own. The loneliness, the awful hurt, the doubts about herself as a woman were washed away as she clung to him and sobbed. It seemed to her she purged herself of the hollow ache that had been a part of her for so long.

After a while she took a shaky breath, her voice very low. "I'm sorry."

"Don't be," he whispered. His fingers gently wiped away her tears. "I'm sorry for making you remember."

His words were fused with such regret and such misery that Gaye raised her head to look at him. His face was filled with tenderness. It wore the same expression it had earlier in the evening when he placed the kiss on Johnny's forehead.

She raised her fingers and stroked his cheek. He shuddered, his arms tightening around her as his mouth moved hungrily against hers. The kiss was long and deep.

His tongue teased its way into her mouth with a loving, tender intimacy. He lifted his head, and his dark eyes searched hers quickly. Then he pressed her face to his shoulder and took a long, shaky breath. She could feel the expansion of his chest against her breast.

"Do you want to tell me about it?" he breathed out softly.

"I'd like to." Her fingers trembled as they clutched the front of his shirt.

With the paradoxical innocence of a child she snuggled against him, and words came tumbling out in sometimes long, sometimes short gasped sentences. Anguished, unconnected words that told of disillusionment and broken dreams and finally of fear for her unborn child. She told how her life had become an awful, torturous, never-ending nightmare until she left Indiana and came to Kentucky to be near her sister. She told of her despair when Mary Ann died and her feelings of guilt when she took another child to her breast. Finally she told of finding this house and the feeling of peace that was beginning to come into her life. Her voice trailed away. She was limp and pliable against him, burrowing against his hardness and strength, his presence healing the old wounds like a balm.

The silence that lingered was finally broken by a crude word that escaped Jim's tight lips. "I'd better never meet that son-ofabitch!"

Her eyes shot up to his face. It was livid with anger. "Don't make me sorry I told you."

He looked back at her, the anger melting from his face. "I had to come along and complicate matters for you, didn't I?"

"Yes. But I don't know if it was all bad." She leaned her elbows on his chest and looked searchingly into his eyes. "You certainly gave me new things to think about." A wave of worry washed the smile from her face. "I'm beginning to love Johnny so much . . . I'm afraid. I don't want to go through all that again!"

Jim caught her upper arms and pulled her over onto his lap. He lifted her legs up onto the couch, and she found herself lying against him.

"I don't want you to be afraid of losing John. I want you to marry me. You can be John's legal mother. He needs you and you need him."

"No. I won't marry for those reasons."

"Couldn't you learn to love me?"

A firm hand lifted her face, and Gaye found herself staring up into dark, serious eyes. Oh, yes, her heart cried, but could you learn to love me?

"You don't *learn* to love a person, Jim. You either love them or you don't."

"You're wrong there, sweetheart. You've learned to love John."

"That's different."

"No, it isn't. Back in the olden days most marriages were arranged, and doubtless to say most of the couples loved each other after a while."

"How do you know? Maybe they hated each other, but had to stay together for the sake of the children. That's probably why so many men had mistresses." Her mouth clamped together stubbornly and she glared at him.

"And you wouldn't put up with that."

"Absolutely not!"

He laughed, clamped her tightly to his chest, rolled, and stretched out on the couch. She lay on top of him. She struggled to get up. He slid one of his legs over hers.

"Jim!"

"Don't panic." He let her go and held both arms straight up. His leg released hers. "I just want to hold you, feel your weight on me. Relax . . . I won't hurt you. Damn, but you feel good!"

"We shouldn't . . ."

"Why not? We're adults."

"That has nothing to do with it. I'm not . . . We're not . . ."

"We're not . . . what?" He chuckled softly. His palm against her head brought her cheek to his chest. She could feel the strong vibrations of his powerful heart. "Have you always been so prim and proper? Don't answer! You have, and I'm glad. I intend to be a strong influence in your life. With me you'll be totally uninhibited." His hand made soothing circles between her shoulder blades. Her limp arm fell over the side of the couch, and a small sigh of pleasure bubbled from her lips.

"Do you like that?"

"Oh, yes!" This was dangerous! Later she'd be sorry. Gaye ignored the warning voice and gave herself up to the intoxicating sensation of being held gently, of not fearing his hands on her body. She felt the tightness of her muscles relax and the strain of long, fearful nights fade into nothingness.

His hand ran up and down her back, slowly stroking, caressing. She turned her face into his shirt, wishing she was brave enough to unbutton the cloth and press her lips to his warm flesh. He shifted his weight; her knees dropped to the couch, and she felt the hard knot of his aroused masculinity. It jarred her out of her lethargy. She put her palms against his chest to push herself away from him.

"Don't let it frighten you," he said softly. "I'm not going to throw you to the floor and have my way with you. Just say you want to leave my arms, and I'll let you go." Her face was so close to his they were almost breathing the same air, so close she couldn't look into his eyes. "I can't help wanting you, I can't help the way my body responds to you, but I can wait. Just don't keep me waiting too long."

It was absolutely unreal to her that she could be here with him like this and he could talk calmly about the hard object pressed to her lower abdomen.

"You can kiss me if you like." His husky voice came to her through the cloud of unreality, and she lifted her head higher to peer down into laughing dark eyes. Suddenly and unexpectedly, laughter burst from her lips. Her hands moved up to his cheeks, scraping across the day's growth of whiskers and into his thick unruly hair. Her fingers closed and pulled.

"Get up and get out of here, Jim Trumbull!" she said between gasps of laughter. "You're strange!"

"Good strange, or bad strange? Never

mind. I don't think I want to know. I want my kiss or I'll dump you on the floor."

"I'll take you with me."

"I'll go for that, if you hit the floor first."

"Don't you wish!"

"Yes! Now stop foolin' around and kiss me. I've got four hours of work waiting for me at home."

Unembarrassed and unintimidated, she eased her mouth up to his. Her lips parted softly as they touched his chiseled mouth. She felt the hand on her back slide to her hips and press her down and upward. His mouth opened under hers. Although he made no attempt to control the kiss, she sensed his growing hunger. It was hotly exciting, unfamiliar. The power of it goaded her to kiss him with a fiery hunger of her own. Her tongue darted through his parted lips to taste.

It was so maddeningly good to have her way with him. She was riding the crest of the wildest, sweetest abandonment she had ever known. Her body moved slowly and sensuously against his, her hair fell down and curtained his face. Her kisses became wetly passionate. The need for air forced her to raise her head and press her cheek to his.

"Oh, God! You're sweet!" His voice was a

breath in her ear. "I want to beg you not to stop, but I don't know if I can hold on to this control I was bragging about."

Gaye took a deep, trembling breath. "I'm sorry. It's not fair to you."

"Let me worry about that." His hands encased the sides of her hips, and he lifted them over to rest on his thigh. "It won't always be like this. Sometime soon, I'm going to kiss you everywhere. I'm almost jealous of MacDougle having these." His palms slid up to the sides of her breasts and squeezed gently.

"Jim . . ." She was suddenly dumbfounded by what she had done.

"Don't be ashamed of wanting me." He lifted her off him and sat up. He smoothed the hair back from her eyes and tilted her chin so she had to look at him. "It's a hell of a time for me to be going away, but I'm already committed. Lady, we've got unfinished business to attend to when I get back. Right now I need a breath of cold air."

He got up and lifted his jacket from the doorknob on the front closet door. Gaye sat on the couch, her hands between her knees. Jim came to her and pulled her to her feet. She walked with him to the door.

"Be careful of that fireplace. Don't build up too big a blaze. And . . . check the doors

— front, back and the basement door — every evening. It'll be a good idea, as long as you're here alone, to keep them locked during the day, too. I'll call you."

He looked at her for a long moment, then bent his head and kissed her on the mouth. It was a soft but lingering kiss. When he lifted his head he checked the night lock on the door, then went out and closed it firmly behind him.

Gaye stood in the window and watched the truck lights disappear down the drive. A shudder of longing worked its way down her body. Two weeks seemed a lifetime away.

CHAPTER SIX

The day after Jim left on his trip, Gaye called a local employment agency and asked them to find her a reliable baby-sitter. She was given the name of a woman who lived a block down the street from her. She talked to several of her references. Convinced she was a responsible person, she called and arranged for her to take care of Johnny for a few hours while she shopped for carpeting for the stairs and upper hall.

Lila Nichols was a divorcée in her late thirties. She had two school-age children and a strong desire to supplement her child-support checks by earning money at home. Gaye liked her immediately.

"Do you have time for coffee before you go?" Lila asked after she had desposited Johnny safely in a high crib, far out of reach of the two toddlers that were left in her care daily. "I get hungry for adult conversation." Her eyes, a bright blue that complemented her dark red hair, were warm and friendly.

"I'd love some." Gaye sat her purse on the dining room table and took off the wool cap that covered her ears. "I wasn't sure I should take Johnny out today. Brrr . . ."

"Julia, darling, don't bother the lady's purse." Lila gave a two-year-old girl a windup toy to get her attention while she gently took the bag from her hands. "You know what? I think Sesame Street is on. You and Adam watch it while I visit with the lady. Later we'll get out the finger paints."

The kitchen was neat, but looked as well lived-in as the rest of the house. Lila poured coffee in mugs and sat them on the plastic placemats on the kitchen table.

"Everything in this house is geared for toddlers," she said with an apologetic laugh. She reached for a big round jar. "How about a chocolate chip cookie?"

"No, thank you. I'm fighting the battle of the bulge."

"You too?"

"I gained thirty pounds when my baby was born. I have about ten pounds to go to get back to what I weighed before."

"Only ten pounds! Right now I'm looking at thirteen!" Lila grimaced down at her jean-covered legs. "I've got drumstick thighs! I'm convinced that I'd have them if

I weighed ninety pounds," she wailed.

"I've never been what you'd call pencil thin myself, but now I'm *too* soft and *too* well-rounded." The instant the words came out of her mouth she wished them back. The image of laughing black eyes beneath thick black brows danced behind lids she narrowed against the flood of memories. Damn you, Jim! Get out of my mind! "I'm determined to get rid of these pounds," she said firmly.

"I've joined an aerobic dance class. The first session is tomorrow night. Want to come?"

"I'd love to! But I'll have to find someone to stay with Johnny."

"Your husband won't do it, huh? Well, mine wouldn't either. He didn't want any of the responsibilities of fatherhood other than providing the kids a roof over their heads and something to eat. His all-consuming interest was climbing the corporate ladder. Oh, well . . ." She sighed. "It's his loss."

"I'm not married and Johnny isn't my baby."

"Oh, Lord. I put my foot in my mouth! I'm sorry."

"It does sound rather bizarre." Gaye

frowned as her mind went back over the events of the past year.

It wasn't until she was in her car on her way to the shopping center that she wondered why she had suddenly confided in Lila. Of course, she hadn't told her the name of Johnny's grandfather or about the relationship that had developed between them. Nor had she told her anything about her own marriage. Only that the marriage hadn't worked out, that she and the man she had married were totally unsuited to each other. Jim was the only person to whom she had ever told the complete story of emotional abuse she had suffered during her marriage. She'd told him things she couldn't even tell Alberta.

Lila had spoken of her former husband with a sadness in her face. They had married young. She'd worked to put him through school. When success came and they could finally afford for her to quit work and have the children she'd always dreamed of having, she discovered he had outgrown her socially and she and the two boys were no longer important to him. He sent the child-support payments regularly, and the boys spent the weekend with him once a month.

Gaye had promised to see if Alberta's

daughter, Joy, could baby-sit Johnny on the nights the dance class met. If so, she would call the city recreational department and join the class.

Thursday morning, as promised, the carpet layers came to carpet the stairway and upper hall. By afternoon Gaye wondered how she could have even considered leaving the floor bare. She brought Johnny downstairs, her stockinged feet loving the softness of the stair treads, and put him in the bassinet while she mixed formula, filled the sterilized bottles and stored them in the refrigerator.

"This time next week you'll be on your own, little man," she told the baby and was surprised by the twinge of regret she felt. "It's best for both of us." Johnny cooed and kicked his feet and looked up at her with his dark eyes. "I've got to wean you away from me in case someone else takes over your care. Oh, baby," Gaye moaned. "You're going to be the spitting image of your grandpa."

The doorbell chimed. "Oh, what now? Did the carpet layers leave a tool behind?" Johnny kicked his feet excitedly. "You like that sound? Well, we'd better go see who it is."

It was the postman with a registered letter. Gaye signed for it, then went back to the kitchen, a puzzled frown on her face.

"Who in the world is Simon, Simon and Litchfield?" Her heart fell to her toes when she read, Attorneys: Louisville, Kentucky. "What's Dennis up to now?" She reached for a paring knife and opened the envelope.

She sat for almost a full minute gaping at the check. *Five thousand dollars.* She unfolded the paper and scanned the curt, businesslike letter. "Client, James M. Trumbull, has authorized payment for care of his grandson, John MacDougle Trumbull, for the past two months. Here after a check for two thousand dollars will be sent on the first of each month. Please present bills for clothing, food, etc., and they will be paid promptly."

Gaye sat staring at the letter and the check for a long while. It was all so impersonal! Jim had put their relationship neatly back into perspective. He was paying for the milk she had supplied from her body, paying for the loving care she had given his grandson. By waving the monthly checks in her face he obviously hoped that she wouldn't be tempted to go out and find a higher-paying job. Tears filled her eyes and rolled down her cheeks. Had he regretted his proposal of marriage and the check was a way to guarantee her services until he could make other arrangements? It was no wonder he hadn't called. He was waiting for her to be impressed by the size of the check!

As the afternoon wore on Gaye was tempted to phone Lila and cancel the dance class. But the more she thought about it, the more determined she was to get out of the house, meet people, and start building the new life she'd promised herself when she came to Kentucky. Johnny and his grandfather had been a detour, she stubbornly told herself, and desperately tried to believe it.

Later she was glad she'd gone to the class. She met two friends of Lila's, both married, childless, and working to make gigantic mortgage payments on their new homes and to pay for the second cars necessary to take them to their jobs. They both confessed they would be bored stiff spending their days with toddlers as Lila did.

The four agreed to meet at a restaurant for coffee before going home.

"What does your husband do?" Kathy, a dental assistant, asked Gaye after they had settled into a booth.

"I'm not married."

"Oh, oh! I guess I asked the wrong question."

Gaye laughed. "No. I'm divorced. I'm . . . baby-sitting for a friend. That's why I have to get home early — because my sitter is a schoolgirl and tomorrow's a school day."

"Baby-sitting? Oh, God! How awful! How do you stand it?"

"If I was cooped up with a baby every day, I'd go mad and bite myself!" added Lila's other friend.

"Beverly!" Lila exclaimed laughingly. "If I had to get dressed up every morning, five days a week, go to the office and put up with that ding-a-ling you put up with, I'd be so depressed I'd eat myself into a size forty!"

"You two girls need to meet some exciting men." Kathy had long blond hair and was continually throwing it back over her shoulder. "We've got one patient that *I'd* go for if I weren't so in love with Gary. Oh, my God! He's like a caveman, but absolutely gorgeous. I wouldn't mind being thrown over his shoulder and carried off to his cave! He's positively the most physical man I've ever met. He'd be just right for you, Lila. I think he needs a woman who would give it back to him tit for tat."

"I'm not interested unless he's rich and

old — got one foot in the grave and the other on a banana peel," Lila said saucily. "My kids are the most important things in the world to me right now. Unless I can find a man who wants to marry all of us, I'll stay single. I've had one man who thought my kids were a bother. I won't ever put them in that position again. Right now they feel loved and wanted. The three of us are a family. That's the way I want to keep it."

Gaye silently applauded Lila. This was a woman with substance.

"Does that mean you won't even date?"

"Date? What's a date? Do you think a man would take me out to dinner and not expect to come back to my place and go to bed with me? Ha! It's happened three times in the last year."

"So? What do you do for sex?" Beverly asked bluntly.

"Without," Lila answered. "My God! The world doesn't revolve around sex. It's a good — no, a wonderful bonus with the right man, but sex for the sake of having sex is a bummer as far as I'm concerned."

"How about you, Gaye?" asked Kathy. "Gary's got a couple of single friends. None of them are anything compared to the hunk I was telling you about. But maybe you don't care for the rugged type."

"I don't mind if he has hair on his chest as long as he has brains in his head," Gaye said lightly.

"Doctor Barker says every female in town from sixteen to sixty has been after this guy for years. He was married once, but that was over a long time ago. I'd say he was fortyish. That's why I thought he'd be just right for Lila."

"Thanks a lot, pal! He'd be too set in his ways for me. Probably hates kids."

"He's got a grandchild. I heard him bragging about him every time the doctor took his hands out of his mouth." Kathy grinned. "Gary knows him. Do either of you want me to play matchmaker?"

Gaye suddenly wanted to be up and out of the booth. She didn't want to stay and hear what Lila had to say. Kathy was talking about Jim, there was no doubt about it! A surge of jealousy swept through her.

"Don't bother on my account," she said when Lila didn't answer. "I'm not ready to be a grandma."

"You might change your mind if you saw him." Kathy raised her brows.

"If he's that great, why not speak for yourself?" Beverly asked.

"I'd never cheat on Gary. But if I did . . ."

"I've got to be going. I told Joy I'd be back

by nine o'clock, and it's almost that now." Gaye gathered up her purse and gloves. She picked up the check. "Treat's on me to-night."

"Okay. I'll treat next time," Beverly said and walked with her to the cashier. "Seriously, if you should want to go out some evening, give me a call. I can always dig up someone for a foursome."

"Thanks. I'll keep it in mind."

Gaye drove Lila to Lila's sister's house. She went inside and returned with two lively boys aged nine and eleven.

"Aunt Betty let us see an R-rated movie," the smaller of the two boys announced as soon as they got into the car.

"She what?" Lila almost shouted.

"You're nothing but a blabbermouth, Kyle," the older boy said with disgust. "It only had violence, Mom. No sex," he continued patiently. "And nothing we haven't seen before. We know the difference between the real thing and make-believe."

"I'm sure you do. But you know the rules and so does Betty." Lila wrapped her arm about Kyle and pulled him close to her.

"Are you mad?"

"Nooo . . . but you know why we go over the TV schedule and mark off the ones you're not supposed to see. The rule applies at Aunt Betty's house as well."

Gaye's respect and admiration for Lila were growing by the minute. She pulled into the driveway at Lila's and stopped behind her station wagon. Somehow, to Gaye, Lila seemed to have it all together. This was a woman with her feet flat on the ground. Despite a bad marriage, she'd hung in there and come out of it with all the things that mattered.

"Here's the key, Kurt. You boys go on in and start getting ready for bed. I'll be there in a minute." Lila gave her older son the key, and the boys got out of the car. "I know you're in a hurry to get home, Gaye, but I wanted to say a couple of things. Don't let Kathy and Beverly pressure you into going out with any of their husbands' creepy friends if you really don't want to go. I've been down that road, and believe me, they wouldn't bring anyone around that was worth knowing."

"Right now meeting a man is my lowest priority," Gaye assured her. "Don't worry. I was burned once. I'm not planning on jumping back into the fire so quickly the next time."

"My sentiments exactly. Not that I wouldn't like to meet the man of my dreams. But I'm about convinced he exists only in my dreams. This caveman Kathy was talking about is probably meaner than a junkyard dog. They usually are after they reach the far side of forty and are still single. If he'd wanted to share his life with a woman, he'd have found one by now."

"Is there a chance you'll ever get back with your ex-husband?"

"None. I've already got two kids to raise. I'm not taking on an immature thirty-seven-year-old!" She swore softly under her breath. "I could kill that man for the way he's screwed up our lives. But enough of that, you want to get going. Shall I come by for you on Tuesday night?"

"I'll call you."

Gaye could hardly wait to get home. She wanted to be with Johnny in the quiet safety of her house. She had expected to spend a couple of hours without Jim occupying her every thought, but even during the class he was there — in the back of her mind.

Wouldn't the girls be surprised to know that she had been held in the arms of the "caveman" who was meaner than a junk-yard dog! What would have happened if she had agreed to a blind date with the "hunk"? It would never have happened. Jim would never allow himself to be manipulated into that situation. Of that she was sure.

Joy, Alberta's teenage daughter, was firmly entrenched in a TV program and reluctantly got up when Gaye came into the house.

"Hi. Have a good time?" Joy asked.

"I guess so. How's Johnny?"

"I never heard a peep out of him. I went up and looked in on him, like you told me to do. He's sleepin' away."

"I'm sorry I'm later than I expected to be." Gaye took some bills from her purse. "Is this what you're usually paid?"

"More than." Joy was a tall girl. She wore straight-leg jeans and boots with heels. Gaye suspected it was the latest fashion at Roosevelt High. "Thanks! Mom said I wasn't to take anything, but . . ."

"If you don't take it, I can't ask you again."

"Well, as long as you put it that way." She stuffed the bills down in her jean pocket and reached for her down-filled jacket. "If Mom calls tell her I'm on my way. She can't get used to the idea that I'm sixteen and have my driver's license."

"Thanks, Joy. One of these nights, if I can get a sitter, I'll come to one of your basketball games. Alberta tells me you're the team's top scorer."

"Only for one game. Mom's exaggerating!"

"Moms are like that. I'll leave the porch

light on until you get into your car. Night."

After Joy left, Gaye moved about the downstairs, checking the doors and turning off the lights. Her eyes sought the drawer where she had shoved the letter and the check that had arrived today. She was tempted to return the check to Simon, Simon and whatever his name was, but they were only acting on the behalf of their client. How in the world, she thought for the hundredth time since she'd received the check, could Jim afford to pay that kind of money for the care of his grandchild! Blacksmithing couldn't be that lucrative!

She looked in on Johnny. She should absolutely refuse to keep him any longer. She knew she should send him away. And she knew she wasn't going to. This baby had filled spaces in her heart that she hadn't known were empty. Spaces her own baby had not lived long enough to fill. Life would be so bleak without him! What would she have left? Nothing!

She undressed while the bathtub was filling and stared with unfocused eyes at her nude body reflected in the bathroom mirror. Six nights ago she had lain on the couch with Jim. Gooseflesh rippled over her arms and legs as she thought of lying on top of his hard, rugged body, her thighs hugged tightly by his, his masculine hardness pressed to her stomach. During that brief time she'd never been so uninhibited, so uncaring for anything except her pleasure and his. Why had it been so natural and easy for her to assert her female prerogative and kiss him like she did?

The shrill ring of the telephone cut into memories of laughter and gentleness, of lips, warm and sensitive, demanding that she share the kiss. Gaye hurried to the bedroom before the ringing could awaken Johnny. It had to be Alberta telling her Joy had arrived home safely.

"Hello." She stood at the bedside table, thankful for the warm, thick carpet beneath her bare feet.

"So you're home." The voice was oozing controlled patience.

"Jim?" Gaye's heart leaped into high gear and pinpricks traveled the length of her naked body.

"Who else? Why in the hell didn't you return my call? I've been waiting for over an hour."

An irrational anger surged through her. "I didn't know I was supposed to return your call. If I had known, I probably wouldn't have done it anyway."

"What the hell are you so mad about? And

what are you doing at a dance class, for chrissake?"

"None of your business, Jim Trumbull, but I'll tell you anyway. I'm taking lessons to become a stripper. I hear there's an opening at Flo's. It won't pay two thousand a month, but I'll have my days free!"

"I don't need any of your smart-ass answers. Didn't the girl tell you I called?"

"No, she didn't."

"I called twice. She said she'd have you call the minute you got home. What are you doing?"

"I'm getting ready to take a bath. Oh, the water is still running!" She dropped the phone and ran down the hall to the bathroom. The water was going out the overflow. She turned off the faucets, grabbed her terry robe from the back of the door and hurried back to the phone. "I'm sorry. I forgot about my bathwater."

"How's MacDougle?"

"He's fine. He'll be completely on formula tomorrow."

"How do you feel about that?"

"Great. It's what I want for him. Which brings up another matter. I got a letter and a check today from your lawyers."

"I thought you'd gotten that weeks ago. Those procrastinating turkeys! Is that the

151

first check you've received?"

"Yes!" she shouted. "And it's the last! Who do you think I am, Jim Trumbull? I volunteered to help you out until you could find a regular nursemaid, and I have no intention of taking that much money for caring for that child. You must think I'm a mercenary bitch!" She paused so she could catch her breath. "If you're so determined to pay that ridiculous salary, I know just the woman for you. She'd be perfect for Johnny. She's got two kids of her own, and she needs the money. As a matter of fact, she just might take you up on the same deal you offered me."

"Are you finished? It's a good thing I'm not there, sweetheart. I'd be tempted to turn you over my knee and pound your butt!"

"Ha! Just what I suspected. When things don't go your way you get violent. I bet you really are meaner than . . . a junkyard dog!"

"What are you talking about? Why is your voice trembling? Are you naked and cold?"

"I'm not naked or cold. I'm mad."

"Oh, for God's sake! I'm the one who should be mad. I've been waiting by this phone and haven't had my dinner yet." His soft laugh was like a wind fanning her anger.

"I'm not at your beck and call just because

I'm taking care of your grandson!"

"Leave MacDougle out of it. There's something special between you and me, and you know it. You still haven't told me what's got your back up."

"It's the money! Dammit! It's so much, it's . . . vulgar, insulting! You can't afford to pay that kind of money, and I'm wondering what you think you're going to get for it."

"Okay. Calm down. Look at it like this. How much would it cost for me to hire a cook, a cleaning lady, a nursemaid, practical nurse, chauffeur, teacher? Do you know how much it costs to hire an English nanny?"

"How would I know a thing like that?" She sat down on the edge of the bed because her knees were shaking.

"I didn't know, either, until I called London and asked."

"You what?"

"I called and found out. Let's forget about this for now. We'll talk about it when I get back. You haven't told me about the dance class. Who did you go with?"

"It's a belly-dance class for women who are *soft and well-rounded* and want to compete in the marketplace for eligible males!"

He laughed, and it was as if his breath was stirring her hair. "You've no intention of letting go of that, have you? Who did you go with?"

"I haven't asked you who you were with this evening."

"Do you want to know? I don't mind telling you. She was a beautiful young thing with long graceful legs, soft brown eyes, a body and a scent that would drive a male wild. She was so busy switching her tail at one male I had a hard time getting on with what I was doing to her." He paused and waited for her to say something. There was silence. "Not funny?"

"Yes, it's funny. It's funny that you're still talking to me when a minute ago you were shouting for your dinner."

"I've missed you . . . and MacDougle." Silence. "Gaye . . . say something."

"Mac— Johnny is beginning to sleep through the night. I gave him a bottle at six. I'll wake him at ten and give him another. That should last him until morning."

"I wish he was still nursing. I'd have a tighter hold on you."

Gaye caught her breath sharply. "Alberta says he's doing fine."

"I know. I talked to her today. I wish I was there. Damn!"

"You'd better go eat your dinner."

"Did you put the car in the carriage

house?"

"I parked by the drive. I think I'll have a yard light installed."

"Good idea. I'll take care of it when I get back."

"No, Jim . . ."

"How come you were so late? The girl said you'd be back by eight-thirty."

"I stopped for coffee with some women I met at the class."

"Who?"

"Have you had your teeth worked on lately?"

"Why do you want to know that?"

"I was just wondering. One of the women works for a dentist. She was talking about getting me a date with an interesting man. She could have been talking about you. The description fit."

"Forget it. My God! Are you considering going out with some guy on a blind date? The man's got to be a loser or he'd get his own woman. Now see here, Gaye . . ."

A bright little devil danced before her eyes. "It would be a foursome. I certainly wouldn't go out with him alone."

"By God! You're not going out with him — period! He's probably a certifiable nut case."

"And you think I'm too stupid and naïve

to take care of myself? Good-bye!"

"Don't you dare hang up until we get this thing settled!"

"Get what settled? I got along without your advice for almost twenty-nine years, Jim. I'm quite capable of managing my life on my own!"

"I'm not sure about that at all! You picked a bastard the first time around and got yourself in a hell of a mess!"

It was as if he had hit her in the face with a bucket of cold water. "You . . . how dare you throw something up to me I told you in confidence!" She had to swallow the sobs of disappointment in her throat before she could continue. "I'm sorry I was foolish enough to confide in you. You're the bastard! I want you out of my life. Do you hear! You — and your grandson!" She was crying. Her voice croaked on the last word.

"Oh, God, babe. I'm sorry. Don't cry. It's only that you can make me so damn mad. I don't understand it. Shhh . . . shhh . . . I wasn't referring to anything except your judgment of men. You're so . . . sweet — so vulnerable. That sonofabitch you married charmed his way into your life. Babe . . . don't cry. Are you still there?"

"Yes, but not for long." She forced herself to swallow past the constriction in her throat. "What you really mean is that I'm stupid and naïve. Dennis may have charmed his way into my life, but you're not going to bulldoze your way into it. I mean it when I say start making other arrangements for . . . for Johnny. He's waking up — I've got to go heat his bottle."

Gaye broke the connection with her finger and placed the receiver on the table. She stood there trembling for a minute that seemed an hour before Johnny's cries stirred her to move.

CHAPTER SEVEN

Dawn finally came.

Gaye had spent the long night hours sorting through every minute she had spent with Jim and through each scrap of conversation that had passed between them. Sleep had come for only a scant hour at a time. She would awaken to lie restless and lonely. Her thoughts were unpleasant company. The sound of his voice and laughter haunted her sleepless hours. "Ah, babe, don't cry." She couldn't remember anyone ever speaking to her so tenderly before — not even her parents, who would have said, "Big girls don't cry."

There were so many things about this man she didn't understand: his wildness, his tenderness. She didn't know anything about his personal life, how he lived, or where he lived. Alberta seemed fond of him, and she was an excellent judge of people.

Damn you, Jim! Get out of my mind. She

got out of bed, drained the cold bathwater from the tub and refilled it with warm. By the time she dragged herself out of the water, her skin was flushed pink. She dried her hair and brushed it into soft waves. She looked at her pale face and reached for some makeup. With a quick motion she dabbed at her cheeks and her lips, then measured the image in the mirror and frowned with displeasure at what she saw. The sleepless night had taken its toll, but what the heck — there was only Johnny to see her, and all that was on his mind was his formula and a dry diaper.

It was nine o'clock before she remembered to place the receiver back on the hook. Shortly after that the phone rang. She was tempted not to answer it, in case it was Jim. Reason prevailed. It could be Alberta.

"This is Karen Johnson, your friendly real-estate agent."

"Hello, Karen." Gaye forced lightness into her voice.

"I've a favor to ask. If it isn't convenient, or if you'd rather not, please say so. There's a gentleman in town who is a relative of the man who built your house. He used to visit there years ago. He's in town for a few days and would love to see the inside of the house once again. I'll understand, Gaye, if you'd rather not give him a guided tour."

"Did you plan to come with him?"

"Certainly."

"What time?"

"Whenever it's convenient for you."

"Give me an hour to tidy up a bit."

"Thanks, love. Bye. See you in a while."

Gaye was almost glad to be wrenched out of her lethargy. She looked around the room, trying to see it with the eyes of a stranger, then moved about quickly, straightening a pillow, stacking magazines and newspapers. She went upstairs, took off the shirt Johnny had burped on, and slipped on a boat-necked knit top. After adding a touch of color to her lips, she ran a brush down over her hair.

Fresh coffee was brewed by the time the doorbell rang, and Gaye put out some sugar cookies she had baked the day before. She'd decided the least she could do for Karen was to be gracious and offer coffee and cookies to the gentleman.

The man with Karen was sixtyish, thin and neat. The black felt hat that sat squarely on top of his white head came off the instant he stepped into the entry.

Karen made the introductions. "Gaye Meiners, Mr. Lambert."

"I appreciate your allowing me into your

home." His handshake was firm and his accent definitely eastern.

"I hope you won't be disappointed in the changes that have taken place over the years."

"I'm sure I won't be. From what I see from here it looks charming." He bent and removed the rubbers from his shiny black shoes.

Gaye hung their coats in the hall closet and led the way through the house. "Would you rather tour on your own, Mr. Lambert? Karen and I can visit in the kitchen."

"I will, thank you." His eyes twinkled. "I remember the house as being much larger. I was just a boy when I was here last. My cousins and I played hide-and-seek from the basement to the attic. Am I invited to have a cup of coffee after a quick look around?"

"Absolutely. I have a young man upstairs who is going to wake up and be very vocal when he discovers his stomach is empty. I'll warm his bottle while you look around."

"Are any of the rooms upstairs off-limits?"

"Make yourself at home." Gaye smiled. "You might peek into the nursery and tell Johnny I'll be up to get him shortly."

"You won't mind? I won't frighten him?"

"Heavens, no! He's a little over two

161

months old, and he'll take all the attention he can get."

Gaye took the bottle from the refrigerator and put it into the microwave. "He reminds me of my father," she said to Karen. "Daddy was meticulous, a refined sort of man. He always put on his coat when he came to the dinner table and stood when a lady came into the room. You don't see many old-fashioned gentlemen anymore."

"Mr. Lambert's that, all right. I really do appreciate this, Gaye."

"I'm enjoying it. I needed something to jar me out of the blahs. But I can't help being puzzled by his wanting to come here. Do you suppose his long-lost love lived here at one time?"

Karen ignored the question and reached for a cookie. "I'd think you'd be so busy taking care of that baby you wouldn't have time for the blahs."

Gaye was thoughtful for a long moment. Is Karen being deliberately evasive about Mr. Lambert? she wondered. Am I imagining it, or is she a little tense this morning? Oh, well, what if the old gentleman does have a deep, dark secret in his past and it's buried in this old house. We all have our secrets and our might-have-beens. She shrugged and smiled.

"What do you know about Jim Trumbull, Karen?"

"Nothing much. Not many people do. The Trumbulls are very private people. I hear he's spending a lot of time here."

Gaye turned away before Karen saw the tremor pass over her face. "He's fond of Johnny. He calls him MacDougle, but I can't bring myself to call him that." The microwave cut itself off, and Gaye took out the warm bottle. "I'll get the baby and feed him if I can persuade you to pour coffee for Mr. Lambert."

When Gaye walked into the nursery, Mr. Lambert was standing beside the crib. He was gazing at the baby, a half smile on his mouth. He seemed to be unaware of Gaye until she came to the crib, and then the smile broadened when he looked at her.

"It's been a long while since I've seen a baby this small. He's a fine boy, Mrs. Meiners."

Gaye let the 'Mrs. Meiners' go by without correcting him, but felt she had to add, "He isn't mine, you know. I wish he was. I'm taking care of him for his grandfather. And he isn't really small for his age. My sister is his doctor, and she tells me he's about average."

Hearing Gaye's voice, Johnny kicked his

feet and waved his arms excitedly.

"He's a handsome, strong boy." There was a slight tremor in the old gentleman's voice.

"Yes, he is." Gaye let down the side of the bed. "You *are* a handsome boy, darling. I'll take you downstairs and show you off to Mrs. Johnson." She picked the baby up and cuddled him to her shoulder. When she looked up she found Mr. Lambert watching her with a strangely intense stare. "Look around as much as you like. We'll have coffee and cookies when you finish."

"Thank you."

Gaye had scarcely settled into the rocker with Johnny snug in the curve of her arm, pulling vigorously on the bottle nipple, when Mr. Lambert came into the kitchen.

"I see you have a fondness for antiques. The rug beater hanging on the wall brought back memories. Who would have thought a rug beater tied with some greens and a ribbon would make such an attractive wall decoration." He sat down at the kitchen table, making himself quite at home, and reached for a cookie. "I haven't had home-made sugar cookies for years."

"I hope you like them. I like to bake, and I also love to restore old things and make them useful." Gaye took the bottle from the baby and held him to her shoulder to burp him. "I enjoy my collection. By the time Johnny is grown up, the treasures will probably be plastic bowls and aluminum pans."

"Do you mind me asking if . . . ah . . . caring for children is your profession?" Mr. Lambert asked hesitantly, as if uncertain of giving offense.

"I don't mind you asking," Gaye answered frankly. "I'm a teacher by profession. I lost my own baby a few days after this child was born. My sister is the baby's doctor, and she asked me to take care of him. He needed . . . a woman's care," she concluded. She was surprised at how open she'd been with a stranger, but she couldn't bring herself to go into details about Johnny's nursing needs.

"You mean the child was left at the hospital for adoption?" Mr. Lambert asked sharply.

"Good heavens, no! Johnny has a grandfather that would fight a bag full of wildcats for him. This baby is wanted and loved, Mr. Lambert."

Gaye hugged the tiny body to her and placed a kiss on the thick black hair. In a small corner of her mind she thought about this polished old gentleman's interest in a tiny baby. He's just being nice, she thought.

It's what's called politicking — he probably wants to come back and bring his family on a nostalgic trip through the house. His voice brought her back to the present.

"I can see that he is." His eyes lingered on Gaye and the baby for a long moment. Then, "You'd better move that plate of cookies out of my reach, Mrs. Johnson, if we're going to lunch this afternoon."

Later, Gaye took Johnny to the living room and laid him on the couch. She stood beside the door while Karen and Mr. Lambert put on their coats.

"It's been enjoyable, Mrs. Meiners." Mr. Lambert held out his hand and shook hers warmly. "Thank you for giving me a glimpse into the past and into the future," he added, almost to himself.

"Thanks, Gaye," Karen said. "I'll call you soon. I've found references to this house in the original plat-book that you may want to see."

"Yes, I'd like to see them. Goodbye."

The house seemed very empty when they left. Normally Gaye would have gone to the kitchen and put the coffee cups in the dishwasher, or put a load of diapers in the washer and started the endless chores connected with caring for an infant. But nothing was normal today. She wasn't even interested in rummaging around in the boxes of antiques Jim had carried to the basement.

Johnny went to sleep on the couch, and she let him lie there. She sat down in the big recliner, picked up a magazine and thumbed through it idly. She saw nothing to catch her interest. Her thoughts were unpleasant company, and the afternoon dragged slowly by.

Late in the afternoon the paperboy came by to collect. When Gaye went to the front door, she noticed Mr. Lambert had left his rubbers sitting beside the door. She tried to call Karen, but the line was busy. Johnny woke fretting because his diaper was wet, and Gaye forgot about calling again.

By ten o'clock she was exhausted, tired both in mind and body. She soaked in a hot tub to ease her tense muscles and crawled beneath the covers on her bed. Her pulse pounded in her temples as she tried to crowd all thought from her reeling mind. Her head was splitting from the pressure, and she pressed her fingers to her temples. Oh, dear Lord in heaven. When would she ever have peace of mind?

Gaye stirred contentedly. A warm, sweet lethargy covered her like a cozy blanket.

Sleepily she wondered about the gentle touch on her cheek and the soft buzzing sound in her ear. She didn't want to wake up. Yet she drifted pleasantly out of a deep exhaustion-induced sleep. Her mind slowly became aware of warm, gentle lips traveling across her cheek and settling on hers. Hers opened invitingly. She tried to lift her arms to hold on to the wonderful dream. It was all so sweet — so deeply real.

She awakened suddenly out of the sweet ecstasy and pulled back in alarm. Panic seized her, and she struggled wildly against the arms holding her. Whimpering, frightened sounds bubbled up out of her throat. Her heart felt like a humming bird gone mad inside her chest.

"Sshhhh . . . babe. It's me . . . Jim. I didn't mean to frighten you."

The sound of his voice penetrated her mind. She was flooded with relief so intense it was almost beyond bearing, and the panic drained out of her. She sank back onto the pillow.

"What are you doing here? How did you get in?"

"I'm here because I couldn't stay away, and I let myself in with the key I took the day I brought MacDougle out to my mother's."

"You scared the fool out of me!"

"I hope so. Because you've worried the fool out of me." He chuckled. His face was so close to hers she had only to turn her head slightly and their lips would touch. "Are you usually such a heavy sleeper? I kissed you a half a dozen times before you woke up."

"I was tired. I didn't get much sleep last night." She moved her head back, trying to see him in the dim light made by the digital clock on the bedside table. His hair was tumbled as usual. It occurred to her then that he was kneeling beside the bed. "You shouldn't be here," she protested in a ragged whisper.

"Why not?" His arm slid beneath her shoulders, and he pulled her to him. "Right here is where I want to be. It's been a week since I held you and kissed you —"

His mouth touched hers softly, gently, and moved against it. There was nothing hurried or demanding about the kiss or the way he held her. She could have backed away and he would have let her go. A sigh trembled through her, and her own lips moved against his, blindly seeking comfort. He lifted his head and rained tender kisses on her eyes, cheek, throat. His hand moved to brush the tangled hair from her brow.

"I want to hold you for the few hours I'll be here," he whispered. "Let me . . . I'll just hold you, if that's what you want." His fingers moved into her hair. He was leaning over her, his lips a breath away. "I *need* to hold you, sweetheart."

A sudden flood of tenderness overwhelmed her. She longed to kiss his lips with sweet, lingering softness, to comfort and hold him, to soothe his brow with her fingertips. She tilted her chin until her lips came in contact with his. The wonder of it, the thought that this big, rugged maverick of a man needed *her,* filled her with pleasure. A fierce feeling of protectiveness came over her. She hugged his shaggy head to her.

He covered her face with kisses. "I was afraid you wouldn't be here. I thought you might have decided to go out with some creep who would've . . . pawed at you, scared you."

"No."

"I'll take you wherever you want to go."

"I'm not real fond of nightlife."

"I'm glad. I'd rather spend evenings here with you." His lips nuzzled her breast before seeking her mouth. His was sweet, his breath warm and smelling faintly of mint. His cheeks were pleasantly rough against her face. His arms were the only arms in the world, his lips the only lips. Something deep within her was stirring. She moved restlessly, a hunger gnawing at her relentlessly.

"Jim . . ."

He pulled away from her and waited. Now is the time to tell him to go, a small voice in her head whispered. There'll be no turning back! In one more minute it'll be too late. She didn't listen. She tugged on the hand holding hers.

Minutes later he lifted the covers, and she moved to make room for him. The bed curved to accommodate his weight when he lay down beside her. His arms reached for her, gathering her close.

His body was hard and warm and big. He cradled her to him with a gentleness that brought tears to her eyes. Gaye felt the tension in her muscles loosen. Reality was fading. The inner qualms were slipping away. He captured one of her hands and pressed her palm to his chest. They lay that way for a long moment, their mouths softly touching.

His hand roamed up and down her back, over her hips, moving the thin cotton cloth of her nightgown. Her fingertips roamed over his chest and smooth shoulders to his neck, lightly fingered his ear and plunged into his wild thick hair.

"You smell good, feel good," he whispered huskily.

"So do you." In a wonder of discovery, her hand caressed his body, finding the corded muscles of his shoulders, the nipple buried in the fur on his chest, the flat abdomen that trembled beneath her touch. Her fingers paused at the top of his jockey shorts and feathered upward.

"Don't stop!"

"Your skin is so . . . smooth."

"Yours is like satin."

"Even the hair on your chest is soft."

"Not as soft as . . . this." His hand slipped beneath her gown. His fingertips lightly combed.

"We sound like kids."

"But we're not. I'm a grandfather and you're . . . sweet beyond my wildest dreams. It's as if I'd never touched a woman's body before. Everything is new and different."

"For me too. Why did you come back?"

"Ah . . . babe. I've had a hell of a day. I hurt you, and I couldn't stand it till I made it right. Can you forgive me for lashing out like a jealous fool?"

"I overreacted. I've never told anyone except you how it really was with Dennis.

And then when I got the check, I felt firmly put in place. When my baby died I was desolate. I don't know now what I'd have done without Johnny. I think Alberta brought us together as much for my sake as for his. I'm beginning to love him very much."

"How about his grandpa."

"Oh, Jim! This *wanting* may not be love."

"It's a damn good start. Don't think about it. I don't want anything to spoil the next couple of hours." His lips tingled across her mouth with feathery kisses. His legs moved apart and braided with hers. "Sweet and soft. I haven't quite figured out what it is about you that draws me to you. I only know I want to be with you all the time. I'm jealous as hell of everything that touches you. Even this." He pulled at the gown and spoke with his lips against her mouth. "I like the way you taste, the way you look, the way you are with me."

"Like now?"

"Especially like now. When you kissed me the other night, I thought for sure my control would snap and I would crush you. I wanted to be . . . inside you so bad."

The arms holding her tightened. She wondered if it was his heart or hers pounding so wildly against her breast. She wrapped her arms around his naked torso. Her ragged breath was trapped inside her mouth by his lips. He rolled so his hand could move up under her gown to her breast. It filled his palm. His strong fingers stroked and fondled as carefully as if he were holding a precious life in his hand. His lips left hers and he gulped for air.

"You were made to be loved and cherished," he whispered urgently. "I'll never hurt you. I'll take care of you always, if you'll let me."

She couldn't speak. Her palms slid over muscle and tight flesh as if she had to know every inch of him. His sex was large, firm, and throbbing against the thigh pinned between his. Strange. She didn't feel threatened by it. She was awed that this giant of a man trembled beneath her touch and yet demanded nothing she was not willing to give.

"Darling . . ." The word came from her lips like a sigh.

He turned her on her back. His bare leg swung over hers and held her softness pinned to the yielding mattress. His masculine scent filled her nostrils. He lowered his head, and she felt the wetness of his tongue through the thin cloth of her gown as he held it to the bud on her breast.

"You mean it? Am I your darling?" He nuzzled the soft mound with his lips.

"Yes! Oh, yes . . . Do you want me, darling?" Her hands slid down over taut hips and pressed his hardness to her thigh.

"More than anything. You?" His hand moved over her body, and suddenly it was there at the mysterious moistness.

"I . . . could get pregnant." She breathed the words in his ear.

"You . . . might not."

"I'm probably fertile as the Nile," she moaned.

"Then you'd have to marry me. Would that be so bad?"

She gave a small, strangled cry. Tremors shot through her in rocketing waves. She grabbed the thick wrist of the hand resting on her belly and pulled the exploring fingers from between her legs.

"I want . . ." It was a quivering whisper.

"Say it, sweetheart! Oh, God! Say it!"

"Yes, yes! Oh, yes!"

A low moan came from him. He supported himself on his forearms, cupped her head in his hands and rained tender, soft kisses on her face.

"Let's get rid of the gown, sweetheart. I want to feel your breasts against my chest, your heart beating against mine."

Her hands moved over his back and down under his shorts. She rubbed her palms over his hips. "If you'll get rid of these . . ."

He claimed her mouth again. She clung to him, her hands stroking his shoulders and back. She was drowning in desire, an emotion she thought never to feel again. He moved away from her as they shifted their weight. In an instant they were back together, naked and straining to feel every inch of each other.

"Even with your arms tight around me, I feel so free."

"I'll never hold you with strength. I'll hold you with love."

"Don't say that!" she whispered urgently. "It's too soon."

"Okay, sweetheart. Okay."

His lips, sweet and firm and knowing, moved over hers. She felt the rough drag of his cheeks, the caressing touch of his wild hair against her forehead. She'd dreamed about being kissed like this, kissed with gentleness and caring. The strength and the taste of him filled her senses. His hand roamed over her back to her buttocks, caressing her into surrender.

"I may be making the biggest mistake of my life, but I don't care," she whispered. "Show me how it could be if we truly loved."

He lifted his mouth and started to say something, then groaned deep in his throat and rolled her onto her back. She gave herself up to his kiss with an abandon that made hunger leap deep inside of him. His hands and his mouth moved down over her body with a velvet touch. His lips captured her nipple, and the rough drag of his tongue was so painfully exquisite, she drew a gasping breath.

"I've wanted to do that from the very first. I'd feel myself growing and I'd breathe deeply and say, Oh, God, don't let me embarrass myself and scare the hell out of this sweet woman. I wanted to take off your clothes and taste every bit of you until you were hot and wet and wanting me. But it's more than that. I want you willingly, wanting me — only me."

"I can't believe I didn't dream you . . ." She wrapped her arms around him, spread her legs so his thighs could sink between hers, and pulled his weight down on her. Cradled together, they rocked from side to side.

He took her mouth in a hard, swift kiss, but the kiss wasn't enough. Only by blending together could they even begin to appease the hunger they had for each other. He lifted his hips. Her hand urgently moved between them to guide him into her.

"Jim . . ." She arched against him in sensual pleasure.

"I'm not hurting you sweetheart?" His cheek was pressed to hers, his words coming in an agonized whisper.

"No! Darling, no . . ." Even now he demanded nothing, gave everything. His concern brought tears that rolled down her face. He turned his head and caught them with the tip of his tongue, then found her mouth and kissed her with lips wet with her tears.

The spasms of pleasure that followed were like a gorgeous dance throughout her body. At times it was like an enormous wave crashing over her. At other times it was like a gentle wind caressing her wet, naked body. The whole world was the man joined to her. His mouth and her mouth were as one. He was at home in her, moving gently, caressing, loving — she arched her hips hungrily and he wildly took what she offered.

It's so wonderful! she thought. The tip of him touches my very soul. I feel so . . . beautiful! She had never known such an exquisite feeling. It was an ecstasy too beautiful for words.

She wasn't really aware of when it ended. When she returned to reality Jim was leaning over her, his weight on his forearms.

"You all right, babe?"

The sweet, familiar smell of his breath, the light touch of his lips at the corner of her mouth, brought a small inarticulate sound from her. She tightened her arms around him, holding him inside her warmth, and hungrily turned her mouth to his. Her hands moved to his tumbled thick hair and fondled his neck and the strong line of his shoulders and back, then came up to stroke his cheeks and caress his ears.

"You're all right?" he asked again when he finally lifted his head.

She laughed softly, caught his lower lip between her teeth and bit gently.

"Yes! Oh, yes." She sighed, then struggled for words to express her feelings. "You've brought me something new. I feel like we've done something wonderful . . . together. I feel filled with you — I think I'll always feel empty without you there." Her breath caught and she couldn't say anything more.

"Sweet, my sweet. You've brought something new to me, too." His lips rubbed hers in sensuous assault. "I want you to feel empty if I'm not there." Their passion swelled, rocked them, enveloped them in a swirling, translucent world where nothing existed but the two of them and the ecstasy they shared.

Afterward, lying side by side, they held each other while their bodies adjusted to the aftermath of passion. Her head rested on his arm; her arm was curled about his chest, her palm flat against his back.

"I wasn't too rough with you, was I? I tried to keep control, but it slipped away and I lost myself in you."

She smiled against his mouth. "You were wonderfully gentle. Thank you. I have never fully . . . participated before. I never imagined it would be so all-consuming."

He gave a deep male sound and his arms tightened. "I could kill that guy!"

"Shhhh . . . no. Now I know how wonderful you are. I'm falling in love with you, Jim. Don't break my heart." Her voice ended in a sob.

He tilted her face up, kissed her deeply. "You're mine, sweetheart. You and Mac-Dougle belong to me."

She believed him. She stretched lazily, her thighs sliding through his hair-roughened ones. "I feel so good. I feel contented and happy. I feel . . . wonderful!" She giggled against his chin and nipped it.

"You are. Believe me, you are!"

CHAPTER EIGHT

"I hate to leave you, but I knew when I came I could stay only a few hours."

Jim sat on the edge of the bed and pulled on his boots. The light from the lamp shone on his hair, and for the first time Gaye noticed silver threads among the coal black. He'd dressed in tan cord trousers, and a soft blue western-cut shirt with pearl snaps was tucked neatly into the waistband. His boots were polished cowhide, and even her inexperienced eye could see that they were custom-made. He looked different. She'd never seen him in anything except jeans, denim shirt, and scuffed boots.

He turned and looked down at her. His eyes possessed a mysterious magnetic force, and she couldn't look away. He smiled, and she felt immersed in a sumptuously delicious joy. She felt as if she were floating several inches above the bed. He bent and kissed her mouth with a demanding pressure.

"This next week will seem like a month." He stood. "I'll use the bathroom and be right back." He paused in the doorway and looked back across the room. Their eyes met, held, and he winked at her.

As soon as she heard the bathroom door close, she sprang out of bed and snatched up her gown. She slipped it over her head and hurried to the closet for a robe. She'd never felt so carefree with another human being, but she shied from the thought of his seeing her naked. She only had time to run the brush through her hair before he returned. He came up behind her, wrapped his arms about her waist, and rested his chin on the top of her head. The breath caught in Gaye's throat. She felt her insides warm with pleasure as she looked at their reflection in the mirror. She had never before experienced this melting, letting-go sensation that invaded her innermost being.

"Don't look at me like that, or I won't be able to leave you." He bent his head and pressed his face into the curve of her neck.

She turned in his arms and slipped hers about him. Her warm, moist lips traced the line of his jaw and moved upward to settle very gently on his mouth, where they moved with sweet provocation. Love and tenderness welled within her. A lovely feeling unfolded and traveled slowly throughout her body. They stood quietly, as if to absorb the feel of each other.

"You must go." Her voice was weakened by the depth of her emotion. "Shall we look in on Johnny?"

They went to the baby's room. Jim's arm was around her, his hand resting intimately on her hipbone. The baby was sleeping soundly. They stood beside the crib. Gaye looked up at Jim with a mischievous sparkle in her eyes.

"You're not like any grandfather I've ever known."

"You're not like any grandma I've known," he teased.

"Will Johnny call you Grandpa?"

"I hope he'll call me whatever *our* children call me — Dad, Pa, old man, hey you —"

Her heart leaped at the thought. "They'll have more respect than that! I'll see to it."

"Yes, ma'am."

Downstairs, Gaye watched him shrug into a shearling coat. He seemed as big as a bear.

"Did you drive down from Louisville?"

"I flew down and got a taxi. I told him to come back about now." Jim looked out the front window. "Here he comes. Come kiss me, sweetheart."

"Will you fly back?"

"Uh-huh." He opened the coat, pulled her against him and lifted her off her feet. He kissed her long and hard. "I'll call you tonight."

"Will you be able to catch a flight at this time in the morning?"

"Don't worry about it. There's a charter waiting for me."

"A charter?" He set her on her feet, and she moved back so she could look up at him. "I really don't know much about you, do I?"

He turned with his hand on the doorknob. "We'll take care of that when I get back. I like to think of you and MacDougle waiting here for me." As he turned, his glance fell on the rubbers beside the door. He gave them a little kick with his booted foot. "Where did these come from? Who's been here?" His words dropped like a bomb. His glittering dark eyes were fixed on her. Hers were fixed on his stern mouth.

"A friend of Mrs. Johnson's left them here. She brought him to see the house." The censorious look in his eyes was so reminiscent of the way Dennis used to look at her when she had displeased him, it cut through her like a knife.

"You let a strange man in the house on that woman's say-so? You don't know anything about her. Why did she bring him here?"

"He wanted to see the house again. He used to visit here when he was a boy. He was a nice man and he liked Johnny, too. Why are you acting as if I've committed a crime?"

"I worry about you and MacDougle here alone." He grasped her shoulders with his two hands. "Trust me, Gaye. Please, be careful about who you let in the house. I wouldn't put it past my former in-laws to kidnap MacDougle."

"They wouldn't send an old man to do it," she said crossly.

"How do you know? You've no idea of what means they'll go to to get what they want."

She stared at him and felt her heart slide to the tip of her toes. "Let's not quarrel," she whispered and tried not to cry.

"I'm sorry, sweetheart." He came to her and hugged her tightly to him. "I want to keep you safe. I've been happier here with you and MacDougle than I've ever been in my life. I want it to last."

"The only thing you have to worry about is stray blacksmiths who have a key to my door," she said and smiled through sudden tears.

The cabdriver sounded the horn. "Oh, hell! Bye, sweetheart." He kissed her as if he wanted to draw her into his body. He whispered something through the kiss that sounded vaguely like, "You belong to me now." His hands were bruisingly tight on her shoulders when he set her away from him. "Bolt the door after me. Sleep in this morning if MacDougle'll let you. You didn't get much sleep tonight." His grin was so endearing her heart almost melted.

Gaye moved to the window to watch the lights of the cab move down the drive. The house was quiet. The only thing to break the silence was the ticking of the mantle clock. She sat down on the couch and tucked her feet beneath the robe. He was gone, and what had happened between them seemed like a dream. Never had she felt so adored, so cherished. Was it possible for him to be such a considerate lover without loving her?

What did she know about Jim other than that he was sweet and gentle, and she had shared the most wonderful experience of her life with him? He expected her to marry him, and she didn't even know where or how he lived. Have I had my head in the clouds? she asked herself. I really don't know him. How can I let him talk about our having children together? Our lifestyles may be so totally incompatible that I won't be able to live with him . . . no matter how much I love him. I don't want to be miserable for the rest of my life!

Long before daylight she had convinced herself that before she allowed herself to be immersed in Jim's life, she had to know more about it.

She was feeding Johnny his morning formula when the doorbell sounded. Holding him cradled in one arm, she went to the door. A shiny black car was parked beneath the portico. Mr. Lambert stood on the step, his hat in his hand. Gaye smiled a greeting, slipped the latch on the storm door and backed away to protect the baby from the cold gust of air that came in when he opened the door.

"Good morning."

"Good morning. Hello there, young man. Are you having breakfast?"

"What stays in him counts for breakfast," Gaye said, laughing.

"I'm on my way to the airport and stopped by to pick up my rubbers. I hear it's snowing in New York."

His friendly smile prompted Gaye to say,

"I thought my sugar cookies had brought you back." He laughed, and it flashed through Gaye's mind that he didn't laugh often. "I have some left, and fresh coffee, if you have time."

"I'll take time . . . if you're sure you don't mind the interruption." He took off his overcoat and laid it over the back of a chair.

"Johnny and I are glad for the company." She led the way to the kitchen. "The cups are in the cupboard on the right and the cookies in the jar on the counter. It isn't often I have to ask a guest to wait on himself, but Johnny needs to finish his breakfast and take his morning nap."

"It's the least I can do. Please carry on."

Gaye heard the clink of the cup in the saucer and the rattle of the lid on the cookie jar as she fed the baby.

"You little . . . stinker! Don't you dare blow! Oh, Johnny, now you're laughing. I think you like to be all messy."

"That's typical of a boy," Mr. Lambert said as he pulled at the creases in his trousers after sitting down at the table.

"He's very alert for his age. Did you notice how his eyes searched for you when he heard your voice? You're a smart boy, aren't you, darling?" Gaye cooed at Johnny and maneuvered the bottle into his mouth again.

"You must love children. First a teacher and now a nursemaid. Do you plan to marry and have a family of your own?"

Gaye looked up to find the sharp eyes fixed on her. If he wasn't such a nice old gentleman she would almost think he was asking these questions for some reason of his own.

"I'm thinking about it," she said slowly, still trying to understand why he wanted to know.

"It'll be a lucky boy who comes home from school to a cookie jar full of these." He took a deep bite of a large, round cookie. A dusting of sugar sprinkled his dark suit, but he didn't seem to notice.

"Do you have children and grandchildren, Mr. Lambert?"

"Yes, I have children, Mrs. Meiners. And I doubt if a one of them can bake sugar cookies." He added the last dryly. Then, as if to change the subject, he said, "I wonder if you would be kind enough to let me jot down the recipe?"

"I'll be happy to share it with you. My mother passed it down to me. I'll take Johnny up to bed and be right back."

When she returned, Mr. Lambert was helping himself to a second cup of coffee.

"Can I pour a cup for you, Mrs. Meiners?"

"Yes, please." She brought her recipe book to the table. "This makes a large batch of cookies. Are you sure you want it?" She smiled up at him. He seems so out of place in the kitchen, but perfectly happy to be here, she thought.

"Absolutely. You should start a franchise and go nationwide."

"Now, that's a thought!" she said with a happy grin. "I can see it now — Gaye's Cookies on the grocers' shelves."

"Don't laugh, young woman. A Kentucky colonel did it with fried chicken." Smile lines deepened the wrinkles in his face. Gaye could tell he was enjoying himself immensely, and the seed of apprehension Jim planted in her mind was pushed to the far corner and forgotten.

"I'll write down the ingredients. Almost any cook will know how to put them together. I always chill the dough before I roll it out and then dip the top of each cookie lightly in sugar and spices before I bake them."

She wrote swiftly and passed the paper across the table. The hand that reached for it wore a large diamond ring. Gold cuff links were visible on the sleeves of his white shirt. The ridiculousness of the situation hit her, and Gaye laughed into his eyes.

His lips twitched into a smile. He reached into his pocket for dark-rimmed glasses and perched them on his nose, then read the recipe. "I should be able to handle that," he said confidently. "I haven't thought of buttermilk in years. We used to have it at home when I was a boy."

"If I don't have buttermilk, I sour a little milk by adding a small amount of vinegar."

"I'll stop on my way from the airport and get buttermilk."

"Don't tell me you can cook!" she teased.

"I can scramble an egg with the best of them," he said with a broad smile. "But my coffee will float a rock." He folded the paper and placed it carefully in his inside coat pocket. "I've taken up enough of your time. Thank you for inviting me to stay."

"I've enjoyed it. When you come back to town, stop by and bring me your recipe for scrambled eggs. Mine are like rubber. Oh, excuse me. I hear Johnny, and he sounds as if he's terribly unhappy about something."

"May I come along and say good-bye to the young man?"

"Of course."

Mr. Lambert followed her up the stairs. The baby's face was red, and he was protesting being left alone in the only way he knew.

"Now, now. My goodness, what's the matter? You're getting spoiled, young man." Gaye picked him up, and the loud wails of indignation ceased immediately. "You rascal, you!" she chided.

"May I hold him? It's been years —"

"If you're sure. He may slobber on you."

"I don't mind." He reached for the baby and held him cradled gently in the crook of his arm, turning from side to side. The look on his face was one of gentle regret. His eyes clung to Johnny's face, and Gaye could see that his jaws were tightly clenched.

He's probably remembering when his own children were babies, she thought, and for a moment she felt a stab of pain in her heart, remembering her own child.

"Thank you," he said simply when he handed the baby back to her.

Gaye laid him in the crib. "Go to sleep now," she suggested softly.

In the living room she held Mr. Lambert's overcoat. He slipped into it. "Thank you," he said and picked up his rubbers. "It's been a pleasure, Mrs. Meiners."

"For me too. Good-bye, Mr. Lambert."

Gaye closed the door behind him and then moved the curtain aside so she could look out. A uniformed man was holding the car door open. A chauffeur had been waiting in the car all this time! For goodness' sake! Gaye shrugged and dismissed it from her mind. She was behind in her work; Johnny's washing had to be done.

Candy, the nurse from the hospital, came by in the evening. Gaye was waiting for Jim's call. She was relieved when her friend stayed only a few minutes, saying she was meeting her sister at the shopping mall.

It was ten o'clock when the phone rang. By that time Gaye was as nervous as if she were waiting for her first date. She laid down the novel she had been trying to read and let the phone ring for the third time while she took deep breaths to steady her nerves, then picked up the receiver.

"Hi, sweetheart. Were you in the bathtub?"

"Ah . . . no."

"I know it's late, but I couldn't get away sooner. Have you missed me today?"

"Of course. Ah . . . Johnny's fine. He seems to be taking to the formula well." She really didn't know what she was saying.

"That's good. . . . I've thought about you all day." There was a long pause, and she heard him make an exclamation of annoyance. "I'm trying to tie up some loose ends here. I'll have to go to New York before I come home, but that'll take only a couple of days."

"New York sounds a million miles away from Madisonville."

"It's only a few hours by plane. Talk to me. What did you do today? Did anyone come over?"

"Candy came over for a short while, and . . . Mrs. Johnson's friend came by on his way to the airport and picked up his rubbers. Nothing exciting. Jim . . . I'm confused. We've got to talk when you get back."

"Confused about what, sweetheart?"

"You . . . and me. Last night I was happy, but today I'm wondering what it all means. Maybe what we feel for each other is just a physical thing."

"Physical attraction is the beginning of most relationships, Gaye. I'd hate for you to love my mind, but hate my body. This didn't happen to me overnight. I was attracted to you from the start. I wish I didn't have to be away from you right now, but this thing in Louisville has been planned for a while. I'm winding up some affairs here." He turned away from the phone and spoke to someone. "Good Lord! All the people do here is party. I wish I was there with you. Are you upstairs in the bedroom?"

"Yes. I've been reading."

"I have to go. I'll call you tomorrow night. What nights do you go to that exercise class?"

"Tuesday and Thursday."

"I'd rather you'd skip that while I'm gone."

"But why, Jim? Joy is a reliable baby-sitter."

"I'm sure she is. It's just that . . . I don't exactly like the idea of MacDougle being there alone with a teenage girl."

"I've already made plans. My friend is picking me up." The sound of the music and the laughter in the background prodded her to ignore the worried tone in his voice. The deep-seated ache in the center of her body, a jealous ache she recognized with reluctant dismay, stirred her to anger. "I'm here during the day. If you can spare a moment you can call then."

"You're ticked off and I don't blame you. But do this for me, sweetheart. Stick close to the house until I get back. You know I wouldn't ask you to do it if I didn't think it a necessary precaution."

The long tense silence was broken by a feminine voice: "Jim, darlin', c'mon."

Anger and resentment came boiling up. "I'm not at your beck and call, Jim. I think I told you that once before. Don't ask me to structure my days and nights to suit your whims. I won't do it. I'm not a child to be told do this, do that. I think you'd better get back to your friends. The party may poop out without you."

Another long pause. "They're not my friends. They're acquaintances. There's a world of difference between the two," he said quietly. Then, "All right. Take care of our boy. I'll call sometime tomorrow. Bye, sweetheart."

"Bye." Gaye hung up the phone and burst into tears.

The weekend passed. Jim called every day. Sometimes the calls came early in the morning and at other times in the afternoon. The conversations were brief and impersonal. She didn't mention the fact that Mr. Lambert had liked her cookies so well he'd wanted the recipe or that he'd sent her a lovely houseplant. They talked mostly about the baby and the weather. He called Tuesday morning while she was feeding Johnny.

"How're you doin'?"

"Fine."

"MacDougle all right?"

"He's fine, too."

"Anything new and exciting?"

"Not unless you think scattered garbage is exciting. Dogs got into it last night."

"Did it snow much there?"

"Several inches. I'm glad I had snow tires put on my car."

"Are you thinking of taking MacDougle out in this weather?"

"Why not? He isn't a hothouse plant. He's got a car seat. He'll be safe enough."

"I was thinking of you, too, sweetheart. I wish you wouldn't go out unless it's absolutely necessary. The roads are slick."

"It snows in Indiana, too, you know. I've been driving on it since I was sixteen." Gaye found her temper rising. What's the matter with him? she fumed. "Don't plan my days for me, Jim. I'm a big girl, I can take care of myself."

"I'm not so sure about that." There was a hard, impatient edge to his voice. "I'm merely telling you driving conditions are bad all over the state. Anyone with any brains at all stays off the roads unless it's absolutely necessary to be on them!"

The quiet hung heavily after he spoke, and Gaye had the inescapable feeling that if he were here he'd be tempted to shake her. She had the mad impulse to feed his anger.

"Evidently I've been functioning without brains for nearly twenty-nine years. That's quite a feat! I've got to go, Jim. You're interrupting our breakfast."

"That's too damn bad! You hang on there

and listen to me! No damn exercise class is worth getting your neck broken!"

"Johnny is your concern, not me!"

"Johnny?"

"Your grandson — little person — tiny hands, small feet! He's blowing formula all over himself. I've got to clean him up. Bye. Call again when you can spare the time."

She hung up the phone. The satisfaction she felt lasted for only a moment. She knew he was right about the roads, and she also knew she had been unreasonable.

In the late afternoon Lila called to tell her the exercise class had been canceled due to the weather. She said her boys had planned on an evening at her sister's and were disappointed. Did she mind if they came over for an hour after dinner?

The prospects of a long, lonely evening had not been pleasant, and Gaye welcomed the opportunity for company.

She checked the cookie jar and decided to make a fresh batch of sugar cookies. When she opened the notebook to find the recipe, she thought of the dapper Mr. Lambert. She wondered if the refined old man intended to make the cookies himself. Impossible! He probably had a housekeeper or a cook. Gaye thought about the look of regret on his face when he held Johnny. What had he been thinking at that moment? He had children, so he probably had grandchildren, perhaps even great-grandchildren, yet he seemed sad. . . . She shrugged the thoughts away and uncovered the mixer.

It had stopped snowing by the time Lila and her boys arrived. They stood in the entry and removed boots and coats.

"It isn't bad driving now. But if the wind comes up, look out!" Lila placed her wet boots on the mat and instructed her boys to do the same.

"I hope the wind comes up." Kyle gave his brother a playful push. "No school."

"Pray, Gaye. Please pray the wind doesn't come up!" Lila pleaded and rumpled the hair of her oldest son. "I've always wanted to see the inside of this house. Oh, it's beautiful!"

"Thank you. I baked fresh cookies, boys." Gaye led the way to the kitchen.

"Eat in here," Lila said when her youngest son started back to the living room. "You'll get crumbs all over."

"Rats! We wanted to watch the fire."

"Let's all go in and sit beside the fireplace. Don't worry about the crumbs, Lila. They'll sweep up."

Later, Gaye found a deck of cards and got the boys started on a game of crazy eights.

"Have you lived here long, Lila?"

"Five years this spring."

"Do you know . . . Jim Trumbull?"

"I don't know him. I've never even seen him, but I've heard of him." She lifted her brows and her eyes teased. "I've heard he stops here quite often."

"It's his grandson I'm baby-sitting."

"I thought so," Lila said with a grin. "But I didn't want to ask."

"Is there anything that goes unnoticed in a small town?"

"Not much. And especially if it concerns Jim Trumbull."

"What do you know about him?"

"Not much," Lila said again. "He lives about five miles out on the county road. He has a gate across the lane leading to his house. It sets back in the timber, and you can't see it from the road. His mother and his aunt live with him. But I guess you know about that. What exactly is the matter with his mother? I've heard a nurse goes out there every day."

"I wouldn't know. He's very closemouthed about anything to do with his personal life." Gaye tried to keep the quiver out of her voice.

"It set the gossips to work when his daughter went into the hospital to have her baby. Up until that time people had forgotten he even had one. I guess he's been divorced for a long time. When his ex-wife came in a chartered plane and took a limo to the hospital to get their daughter, their tongues worked overtime. I've never heard anything *bad* about him, Gaye. He's probably just a nice person who values his privacy. That's as much as I know about him except that I heard he isn't exactly poor. You can't blame him for that."

"He can't be rich. He's a blacksmith. He wrote a book about it."

"A blacksmith? I've never heard that. I heard he has some weird iron sculptures out at his place and an assortment of animals, including some very fine horses, but I haven't heard of him being a blacksmith."

"Oh, well, it doesn't matter," Gaye said tiredly.

The phone rang. She excused herself and went to the kitchen to answer it.

"I'm at the airport in New York. I just got in." Jim's voice. Somehow she felt unreasonably irked that he should call while they were discussing him.

"I'm having coffee with a friend."

"Who?"

"The dance class was canceled so my

friend from the class came over," she said irritably. "Did you think I was entertaining someone from the Mafia?"

"No I didn't think that. I'm interested, that's all."

"She's perfectly respectable. Her two sons are with her."

"I'm glad you have someone to keep you company this evening. Gaye, about this morning . . ." The placating note in his voice irked her even more.

"You acted as if I'd take Johnny out in a blizzard and risk his life on unsafe roads. I'm surprised you think I'm even capable of taking care of him." The anger she was feeling echoed in her voice. Oh, good heavens! she thought. I'm acting like a shrew and I can't stop!

"I ask you to exercise a little caution. Is that too much to ask? Did you have a bad day?"

She wanted to say, Hell, yes! Every day you're away is a bad day. Instead she said, "It was all right." Her throat felt as if it had a rock in it.

"I've missed you."

"Oh, sure."

"Dammit, Gaye!" he bellowed. She moved the phone from her ear and let it rest on her shoulder. His patience snapped. His anger and frustration seemed to surge up and boil out. She caught snatches of angry words. "If I was . . . smart-ass answers . . . damn mad . . . what the hell are you trying . . . unreasonable! By God . . . give you a damn good . . . Now you listen to me. . . . I've had about all . . . enough on my plate without you. . . . Are you . . . to . . . or not?" There was a kind of desperation in the jerky way he spoke. "Answer me, damn you!" he shouted, and his tone savaged her, sending shivers of anxiety down her spine.

"How can I answer when you keep shouting? You must be making quite a spectacle of yourself at the public phone booths."

"To hell with the spectacle I'm making of myself. Who the devil cares? It's you and MacDougle that concern me."

"If all you're going to do is shout at me when you call, then don't!" She heard a muffled curse and scraped up enough courage to say, "I refuse to be dominated by you or anyone else, Jim. I won't be told when to breathe and when not to. Even Alberta gives me space, and I'm a lot closer to her than I am to you."

"There is no one in the world closer to you than I am," he said, and his voice was surprisingly calm. "No one has a greater right to look after you than I do. Oh, hell!

I'll call tomorrow. Good-bye."

Gaye stood for a moment after the connection was broken. What she really wanted to do was crawl in bed and cry; instead she put a half smile on her face and went back into the living room.

Thursday night she went to the dance class, but declined the invitation for coffee at a local restaurant later. When she returned home Joy didn't mention having received a telephone call, so she asked her as she was leaving.

"Were there any calls?"

"No. Were you expecting one?"

"Not really. By the way, congratulations on making the honor society."

"Thanks. Will you be needing me next Tuesday?"

"Sure, unless you have something planned?"

"I've got something planned all right. I want to go to France next summer with a group of French students. I need to earn money."

"You can count on steady employment here."

"Thanks, Aunt Gaye. See ya soon."

Gaye closed and locked the door. Two days had gone by without a call from Jim.

CHAPTER NINE

A week went by. The wet, dirty snow was covered with a clean blanket of white. Thanksgiving came and went. Christmas lights began to appear. *Twelve days without a word from Jim.*

Lila called on Tuesday morning. "Will you drive tonight? I know it's my turn, but my old bucket of bolts is being stubborn again."

"Sure. I'll pick you up at the regular time. Johnny and I went to my sister's for Thanksgiving, and I tried to eat 'the whole thing.' I feel lumpy and pudgy, but I enjoyed every calorie."

"Christmas is coming on," Lila moaned. "I'll be big as a house by New Year's Eve."

Gaye forced a laugh. "I doubt that."

"Oh, say, the captain of the neighborhood watch program called last night. There's been a strange blue car in the area for the past week. He asked me to pass the word along. It's nothing to be alarmed about. I don't get too excited about these reports. Someone probably has out-of-town relatives visiting for the holidays."

"You're probably right, but I'll pass it along to the sitter. See you tonight."

Gaye had spent the long days refinishing the primitives she had brought from Indiana. She carried them up from the basement a few at a time and worked on them in the kitchen so she could be near Johnny. At night, if sleep wouldn't come, she would read or turn on the television and watch the all-night movie channel.

When each dawn came she would ask herself the same question. Why had she fallen in love with Jim Trumbull? Why had her body responded to his and longed for him, as it did even now? Why did the sound of his whispered words haunt her sleepless hours, and why couldn't she forget the pleasure that had flowed between them?

Each night she asked herself, why is he staying away? Will he call tomorrow? She also had begun to question her own stability. In a year's time she had fallen desperately in love with two different men who were as unlike each other as day and night.

She didn't know what she would do without Lila's friendship. They talked to each other at least once a day on the telephone.

Being confined to the house with children, Lila was forever needing something from the supermarket that Gaye dropped off after she finished her own shopping.

Gaye spoke to Alberta daily, but her sister was a busy woman and Gaye tried not to take up time Alberta could spend with her teenage children.

Johnny was developing a personality of his own. It hadn't taken long for him to learn that the more noise he made, the more attention he received. Gaye dressed him in the denim overalls she had bought for him and took him to the photographer. He proved to be a regular ham — loving the lights and the noise — and she was sure the pictures would be adorable.

Gripped by her need to clear her mind of thoughts of Jim, Gaye threw herself into the exercise routine with vigor. She let the music envelop her, let her ears hear only the voice of the instructor.

"Two, three, four . . . higher, higher. Pull those muscles, girls. One, two, three, stretch. Keep the legs straight, Lila. Two, three, four, touch the floor, Kathy." Gaye felt her heartbeat accelerate, felt the muscles pull, felt the power of the music forcing her to keep pace with it, felt the sweat trickle down between her breasts.

"On the floor, girls. We'll level off with something slower. You've lost weight, Gaye. I'll have to use you as an advertisement for my class. Here we go. One, two, three, four, stretch and hold . . ."

Gay scarcely heard the instructor call her name. The song, "Bridge Over Troubled Water," flowed out of the speaker. It was one of her all-time favorites. I won't cry, she told herself sternly. I won't. Dear Lord, she prayed, let me get over him. Please . . . let me not care.

After the class she peeled off her sweat-soaked leotard, showered and dressed. While she was waiting for Lila, Barbara, the instructor, called to her.

"You're looking great, Gaye. You've really lost weight."

"I hadn't noticed. I haven't weighed myself lately."

"Not weighed yourself lately?" Lila came out of the dressing room and echoed her words. "If I pass up a doughnut, I run to weigh myself to see if it's made a difference. It isn't fair!"

"When they passed out fat, I got a double helping, too," Barbara said, laughing.

Gaye wondered where in the world the

tiny instructor had put the extra helping of fat.

"Kathy and Beverly want to stop for a drink. Is that okay with you, Gaye?" Lila looked hopeful, and Gaye shrugged indifferently. "Would you like to come along, Barb?"

"No, thanks. I've got a husband and two boys at home. They've probably got the house torn apart by now. I'll see you next week."

Gaye would rather have gone home, but she didn't want to disappoint Lila. They followed the women in the other car to a nightclub. The outside of the building looked like a warehouse; the inside looked like an exclusive restaurant and bar, which it was.

They paused in the entry to allow their eyes to become adjusted to the dim light, then Kathy led the way to the bar. They sat at a round table in padded barrel-back chairs. Gaye reminded herself to be pleasant, to smile, to not act as if she'd rather be anyplace else in the world but here. She ordered rum and Coke.

"I love it here. They serve the most fabulous lobster." Kathy was definitely in her element. "What do you say we treat ourselves to a night out when we finish the class."

"What? And put all that weight back on? I wonder if they have a salad bar?" Lila giggled.

"If they did, it would cost an arm and a leg. You might as well go for the lobster."

"Speaking of 'go for' — isn't that your caveman coming out of the dining room with the tall blond?" Beverly stretched her neck to get a better look.

"Damned if it isn't! Look, Lila. Isn't he gorgeous?"

Gaye knew who they were talking about even before her eyes landed on the big man in the dark suit. Her heart dropped to the pit of her stomach, and she felt the blood drain from her face. She glanced quickly at Lila and found her staring at her. She shook her head in a silent plea, and her friend nodded. Gaye sat stone still, as if the slightest movement would cause him to look her way, and thanked God that they were sitting in the darkest corner of the bar.

"I wonder who that is with him. I haven't seen her around here before. I'd remember the clothes, if not the woman."

"She's no sweet young thing. She looks more like a member of the Four Hundred Club. God, he's handsome! Mature! Rugged! How'd you like to go to bed with a hunk like that? I bet he's like a leashed stallion!"

"You can talk, Kathy, but if he made a pass at you it would scare you to death." Lila reached for a cocktail napkin and wrapped it around her glass.

Gaye couldn't take her eyes off the couple across the room. He'd had a haircut. His hair had been *styled.* These thoughts came to her among others: the white shirt makes his skin look darker, and the suit is tailor-made to fit his broad shoulders. The woman with him acts as if they've known each other forever and that he belongs to her. Oh, God! Why did I come here tonight? Gaye, you fool. This hurt reaches into your very soul. It was never like this with Dennis.

Jim helped the woman into a long fur coat and took her arm, and they passed out of Gaye's sight. She sat numbly, grateful for Lila's chatter. The other two girls launched into their plans for a Christmas skiing holiday. Gaye pretended to listen, nodded occasionally, and when she finished her drink refused to order another.

"No more for me, either," Lila said. "I'd just as soon head 'em up and move 'em out toward home. I don't know, Gaye, if we should leave these two lambs here for the wolves or not."

"I think they're capable of handling most anything that comes along," Gaye said lightly. "Have fun, you two."

Lila didn't speak until they were in the car and on their way to her house.

"What gives, honey? I saw your face when you saw Jim Trumbull. That was Jim Trumbull wasn't it?"

"Yes, it was him. I thought he was out of town. I haven't heard from him for a while, that's all. I guess I was just surprised to see him dressed up." She laughed and prayed it didn't sound too forced. "He didn't look like the same guy."

"Are you going to continue taking care of his grandson?"

"That's a decision I have to make before long. If I want to teach in this school district next year, I should be putting in my application." Gaye turned the car into Lila's driveway. "How come the boys didn't go to Betty's tonight?" she said, desperate to change the subject.

"Kurt thinks he's old enough to baby-sit Kyle. Tonight is a trial run. I see the house is still standing, so maybe he is old enough. Talk to you tomorrow." Lila got out of the car with a wave of her hand.

Gaye drove slowly down the block. Her

shoulders slumped, her lips trembled on muttered words. "Jim, you monster! Why didn't you tell me you were coming back? And why did I have to see you with that woman! I could have handled it without that!"

She passed Joy's little car in the driveway and drove around to the carriage house. The new yard light lit up the area, and she was no longer afraid of the walk to the side door. One more hurdle to cross, she thought as she closed the garage door. Get Joy out of the house and I can sit and think about what I am going to do.

Joy left immediately after stuffing the bills in her pocket. "I never heard a peep out of Johnny, Aunt Gaye," she said at the door. "See you next week."

Gaye stood in the middle of the room and listened to Joy rev up the motor and shoot off down the drive. Then she removed the fire screen and put another log on the fire. She padded through the house in her stocking feet and turned out all the lights except the small one in the hall, then slumped down in the recliner.

She didn't know how long she had been sitting there listening to the crackling fire eat up the log. She thought about taking some aspirin or a bath, but she did neither.

She sat quietly, scarcely moving a muscle. There was a numbness inside her, a disappointment so great Gaye couldn't put a name to her emotion. The doorbell chimed, and she lifted her feet off the ottoman with regret. Joy had, more than likely, forgotten her schoolbooks.

Gaye switched on the lamp beside her chair and reluctantly went to the door. She flipped on the outside light, unlocked the door, and opened it.

Jim stood on the steps, his hand attached to the elbow of a tall blond woman in a hooded fur coat. He wore his shearling coat and his head was bare. His hair was no longer neatly combed, but wildly wind-blown. She stared at them blankly as she wrestled with the conflicting emotions that stormed through her. Resentment, anger . . . love; they were all there, beating against the wall of her heart. Her first impulse was to slam the door. How could he do this to her? The deceitful, conniving jerk! Jealousy ripped through her with biting pain. Then pride took over and gave her courage a needed boost.

"Good evening, Mr. Trumbull." Her calm voice and placid expression masked the wrenching ache that tore at her heart.

"Hello, Gaye. I know it's late, but we came

by earlier and saw that the baby-sitter's car was here. We drove around awhile and —"

"And you want to see your grandson. I understand. Come in." Gaye stepped back and swung open the door.

The first thing she noticed about the woman was the perfume; the second thing was how tall she was.

"Gaye, this is Jean Wisner. I've talked so much about MacDougle, she thinks he's unreal and wants to see him for herself."

"He's definitely real," Gaye said carefully and was proud her voice was steadier than her stomach. "May I have your coat?"

"Thank you, but we won't be staying that long," Jean announced as if she were speaking to a butler or a maid.

Jim frowned and shrugged out of his coat in what seemed to Gaye a deliberate contradiction of his lady friend's words. She threw him an impatient glance.

His presence filled the room. Gaye moved quickly to the other side of the couch. She hadn't looked at him since her startled eyes had met his when she opened the door. She could feel them on her now. She felt warm, almost suffocated. Her throat hurt, and she swallowed before she spoke again.

"I'll take you up to see Johnny," she said and moved toward the stairway. She'd be damned if she'd let them wander about in *her* house alone! "He sleeps through the night. He's one of the rare babies who never gets his days and nights mixed." She knew the woman was directly behind her when she started up the stairs. The perfume! Phew! She hated strong, sweet scents — it was the reason she used unscented cosmetics.

"Johnny? I thought his name was Mac-Dougle," Jean corrected her.

"Mr. Trumbull calls him that, but his name is John MacDougle. While he's in my care I like to think of him as Johnny." Gaye was proud of the fact that she was able to respond coolly to Jean's thinly disguised thrusts.

Gaye stepped inside Johnny's room and turned the round switch beside the door, making the dim light brighter. Jean went immediately toward the crib. Jim paused in the doorway. Gaye tilted her head and looked up at him. The heady bliss she had shared with him was being destroyed bit by bit. She felt as if the licorice black eyes beneath the thick, straight brows were reading her innermost thoughts, attacking the barrier she had erected to protect her pride.

They exchanged a charged look before Jim's eyes released hers and he moved toward the crib. Her eyes, filled with the awful hurt she refused to allow him to see, followed him. He bent over and lifted Johnny, swinging him up into the crook of his arm.

"The little devil is awake, Gaye." He looked back over his shoulder. His face was beaming with pride. She prayed the wretchedness she was feeling wasn't reflected in hers.

"He's beautiful! Adorable!" Jean held out her arms, and Jim let her take the baby. "You're a darling," she cooed.

Johnny's face puckered, and he let out an earsplitting cry of terror.

"He's frightened!" Gaye moved almost without being aware of it and snatched the baby from the fur-clad arms. She turned her back on the two startled people beside the crib and cuddled him to her. "It's all right, darling. Sshhh . . . don't cry. No one is going to hurt you. Sshhh . . . ," she whispered reassuringly. Johnny gasped a few times, and then his crying ceased as abruptly as it started. "There, there . . . you're all right."

"It's my fault. I shouldn't have tried to hold him." Jean moved over beside Gaye and looked anxiously at the baby.

"He isn't used to strangers," Gaye said,

more sharply than she knew.

"I can see that. I'm sorry I frightened him." She took hold of a tiny fist and Johnny spotted the large, sparkling diamond on her finger. He grabbed for it, a grin splitting his toothless mouth. "I think he's decided he likes me. Do you think he'll let me hold him now?" Gaye released the warm little body reluctantly. The instant Johnny felt himself being transferred from Gaye's arms he let out a cry of rage. Jean shoved him back at Gaye and stepped back. "I'm afraid you're going to have a mama's boy, Jim," she said impatiently.

"What's so bad about that? MacDougle feels safe with Gaye. She's his security."

"You shouldn't allow him to be so dependent on one person. Each time you change sitters, he'll have to adjust. He needs to know that any number of people will look after him."

Gaye went pale. Her eyes quickly sought Jim's face. He looks tired, she thought. The hard bones of his jaws were clenched, and there were shadows under his eyes like bruises. The lines on each side of his mouth were lines of fatigue. Her breath caught in the back of her throat. He was watching her through half-closed lids.

"MacDougle needs to get back to sleep.

C'mere, laddie. You're not afraid of me."

Jim came close to Gaye. His hand moved caressingly down her arm to cover hers as it cupped the small bottom. She felt the pressure of his fingers squeeze gently before he lifted his grandson to his shoulder. Johnny grabbed a handful of Jim's hair and held on. His other hand flayed at Jim's face.

"Hey . . . there! You learned a few tricks while I was gone." He bounced the baby in his arms, and the infant giggled.

"He knows you, all right. You must spend a lot of time with him." Jean's face swung toward Gaye, her gray eyes appraising. Gaye could feel the intensity of envy within them.

"I spend as much time with him as I can." Jim deftly put his grandson in the crib.

"I see you've done this before." Jean moved to the doorway and turned to look about the room. "He'll need more space than this before long."

A sudden knifelike anger stabbed through Gaye. "Mr. Trumbull will be making other arrangements for him soon, Mrs. Wisner. Perhaps you'd like to take on the job. It pays well." The patronizing tone in her voice fit perfectly with the tilt of her chin.

Jean looked down at her coolly from her superior height. "I could handle it. I have a big house and reliable household help.

That's an idea, Jim. Bring him out to Bowling Green and I'll look after him for you."

Jim's dark eyes were on Gaye when he spoke. "Thanks for the offer, Jean, but the boy stays here . . . with me." There was a finality to his statement, and Jean flounced from the room.

Gaye turned down the light and followed them down the stairs. At the bottom she paused on the last step and found herself looking into a ruggedly handsome, amused face. The twinkle in his eyes infuriated her and frightened her. Her heart gave a sickening leap. The big jackass knew she was jealous!

"I like the stair carpet, Gaye."

"I'm glad, because you paid for it," she replied with an indifferent composure she was far from feeling.

"It's rather warm in here. If we're not going, I'll have to take off my coat." Jean's impatient voice cut between them.

"We're going," Jim said softly, still looking at Gaye.

Her head was pounding. She was unable to get her thoughts together. She was tired and confused and wanted them to get the hell out of her house before the plastic expression on her face cracked and crumbled. She felt limp and as drab as a pile of wet laundry beside this willowy, perfectly groomed, confident woman. Her only defense was to force her thoughts inward. Play the game, Gaye. Be perfectly polite. If you break down, he'll know he's gotten to you. She stepped around Jim and went to the door.

"Are you all right, Gaye? You look tired."

"I'm fine, Mr. Trumbull. You?"

"Fine."

"You're dead tired, darling." Jean pulled the hood of her coat up and arranged it carefully over her perfectly coiffured head. "I know for a fact you haven't had much sleep since we left Europe. Not even you, darling, can go three days with a couple hours' sleep."

Gaye pulled open the door. "Good night."

"I'll be back," Jim said as he passed her.

She resisted the impulse to slam the door behind them and immediately switched off the outside light. "I hope you fall down the steps and break your fool neck!" she muttered. "You'll be back, all right! Damn right, you will!" A wave of self-pity washed over her. Why did it have to hurt so damn much?

Gaye drew a warm bath and tried to soak away the feeling of hurt and disappointment inside her. She was nervous and jumpy and on leaving the tub slipped into her gown and went into the baby's room. He was sleeping soundly. Her fingers gently stroked his head and the tears finally came. A deep, shuddering sigh convulsed her body as the questions throbbed in her brain. To give Johnny up now would be like giving up her own baby all over again. How could she bear it? Would Jim come for him in the morning?

Jim. She didn't want to remember how tenderly he had made love to her. The hellish nights she'd spent with Dennis were like a black cloud, and the time she'd spent in Jim's arms was the silver lining. She stood beside the crib and weighed the pros and cons. She could continue to take care of Johnny if she wanted to. In spite of everything, she was certain that Jim wanted what was best for his grandson. But could she do it? No, she decided. It would be better to make a clean break. Better for her and better for Johnny.

She went to her room, crawled wearily into bed and pulled the coverlet up over her ears. She drifted into a sort of trance. Sleep eluded her for what seemed hours. Finally a deadly lassitude crept over her and she slept.

She awakened suddenly. The telephone was ringing. Frightened, she sat up and reached for the light switch. The light sprang on, and she squinted against its harshness, searching for the phone with sleep-drugged eyes. Just as her hand found it she realized it wasn't the phone, but the doorbell. Good Lord! It must be Jim — he said he'd be back.

Gaye sat on the edge of the bed, fully awake. She wouldn't let him in. He could come back in the morning. But . . . maybe it wasn't Jim. It could be an emergency — Alberta! She grabbed up her robe and crept down the stairs. A long dark car was parked beneath the portico. *Bang!* The door rattled beneath the heavy pounding.

"Open the door, Gaye. I know you're there. I saw the light go on in your bedroom."

It *was* Jim! No! she screamed silently. I can't face you tonight. She stood slumped against the wall, her heart galloping in her breast while a thousand tiny hammers pounded her head.

"Let me in. I want to talk to you."

A sharp rap caused her to jump back. Had he lost his mind? He was making enough noise to wake up the whole neighborhood.

"Open the door! Dammit! I'd be in there if it wasn't for that goddamn bolt!"

"Go away, Jim. We can talk in the morning."

"We'll talk now!" he shouted. The pounding that followed jarred the windows.

"You're waking the whole neighborhood."

"I know how to really wake them up. I'll get in the car and sit on the horn. That ought to do it."

Should she let him in and get it over with? While she was trying to decide what to do, automobile lights flashed in the room. A car came swiftly up the drive and screeched to a halt.

"Hold it right there!" an authoritative voice commanded. "Hands up. Turn around."

The police? Oh, dear heavens! Gaye leaned weakly against the door. She'd forgotten about the neighborhood watch program. She turned on the outside light and opened the door.

"Who are you and what're you doin' here?" Two uniformed policemen confronted Jim.

"Jim Trumbull, Officer Callaway."

"Jim? What the hell are you doin'? We've had at least five calls reporting everything from a break-in to disturbing the peace."

"My lady friend is a heavy sleeper!" Gaye gasped at the implication of his words. Jim turned. "There you are, darlin'. Were you going to make me sleep in the car tonight? I'd much rather sleep with you."

"You . . . jackass!" Gaye felt sick, filled with humiliation and self-contempt for what she had allowed to happen, which gave credence to what he was saying. She stepped back and tried to slam the door. Jim moved quickly and stuck out his booted foot.

"Oh, no, you don't. Calm down, sweetheart. I know you're mad at me, but I'll make it up to you. As you can see, I've got my work cut out for me tonight," he called laughingly over his shoulder to the officers.

"Okay, Jim. See you, 'round."

"I don't want you here," Gaye protested, but Jim pushed her aside, came in, and closed the door.

"Hush up and turn on the light."

Gaye numbly moved through the gloom to the lamp beside the chair, switched on the light, then headed for the stairs. Jim's roar halted her.

"Gaye! I'm almost dead on my feet and my temper's on a short fuse. We'll talk here or upstairs; it's up to you."

Gaye turned and looked at him. A kind of brittle calmness possessed her. He was taking off his coat. He still wore the dark suit, but the tie was loosened and hanging askew. He looked tired and haggard, but she refused to soften toward him.

"I made a mistake the other night when I allowed you to stay. I've no intention of making that mistake again. So if that's what you're here for, you might as well leave."

She knew her biting words affected him. His lips tightened, and his brows drew together in an ominous scowl.

"Make some coffee. This is going to be a long night."

"We can talk in the morning."

He ignored her words. She watched him take off his suit coat and toss it carelessly aside, take off his boots and place them beside the chair. He went to the fireplace, and carefully and methodically, he began to arrange shredded paper and kindling to build a fire.

"Jim . . ."

"Dammit, Gaye! Can't you do this one thing for me without arguing?" The scowl on his face made him look older and more fierce.

He was very angry! Feeling more panic-stricken than she ever had in her life, Gaye almost ran to the kitchen.

CHAPTER TEN

"I saw you at the bar tonight. Do you make a habit of stopping there?" He was sprawled in the recliner, his feet on the ottoman.

The attack hit Gaye like a dash of cold water the instant she came into the room. She paused at the end of the couch, then set the coffeepot and mug on the table beside his chair. She answered him with a question of her own.

"Does that make me unfit to care for your grandson?" She sat on the end of the couch and curled her feet up under her robe.

"You saw me there with Jean. Why don't you say it?" He was staring at her. Her eyes flew to him, then just as quickly darted back to her tightly clasped hands in her lap.

"Yes, I saw you there. How was Europe?"

There was a long pause, and she thought that either he hadn't heard her or he planned to ignore her. Finally he said, "I didn't notice. I was there on business."

Then, with his dark eyes fixed firmly on her face, he asked, "What were you doing at the bar?"

"What does one usually do at bars?" she said flippantly, unaware of the stricken look on her face. The silence between them was heavy and deep. Her eyes moved from him to the floor. For a moment she was incapable of speaking. Then anger stiffened her spine. "Can you think of a better place for a single woman to make friends?"

"If I thought that was true, I'd —" he snarled.

"You'd what?" Gaye jumped to her feet. Her face paled. "I think this has gone far enough, Jim. I don't have to sit here and be insulted in my own house. I want you to leave." His glittering dark eyes blazed into hers. She gazed at him blindly, waiting, her own eyes fixed on his hard, sensual mouth.

Suddenly the anger left him. "I'm sorry," he said wearily. "Sit down and talk to me. I've been worried sick. The last ten days have been pure hell." He held her eyes with his. Now he could see the ravages in her face, ravages no cosmetics could disguise. Her cheeks were hollow, her skin so pale it seemed transparent, her brown eyes, usually so soft and shining, bruised and sullen. "You've lost weight."

"Don't change the subject!"

"Okay. I've got a million things to tell you, and I don't know where to start. I went to Europe to see Marla, got stuck with Jean — oh, hell! I can't lose you and MacDougle!" he blurted. In the silence that followed he rested his head against the back of the chair and closed his eyes.

Gaye's body tensed as she tried to stop trembling. She sank back down on the couch, her eyes fastened on his face. He confused her, excited her, angered her. Wisps of dark hair lay on his forehead, matching eyebrows that were as thick and straight as if they had been put there by the stroke of a paintbrush. There was a tension and vibrancy about his body that made her think of a coiled spring. The tightness in her stomach worsened; her eyes misted, blurring her vision. The tension had made her lightheaded.

"I've known Jean for ten years. We were involved in a business venture together. That's over now," Jim said quietly.

He'd been so still and quiet she had thought he'd gone to sleep. Now she realized he'd been watching her through shuttered lids. Somewhere in a quiet little corner of her heart she felt a stab of pity for him — he seemed so weary.

"She doesn't want it to be over," Gaye said with a weary sigh of her own. "She's in love with you."

"She only thinks she is." Jim spoke completely without vanity. "Jean would be bored with me in no time at all. She only wants what she can't have. We'd never hitch together. She'd make a lousy mother for MacDougle, for one thing. The other, and the most important reason I'd never marry her is that I'm head over heels in love with someone else."

"If you mean me, Jim, I'm not buying it." There was a slight tremor in her voice when she spoke, but her eyes met his unwaveringly.

"I do mean you, Gaye. And I'm going to do everything I can to see that you buy it. We should have had this talk the night I came back, but I didn't want to worry you. Besides, I had other things on my mind that night." The change in his face was magical. A soft, loving light shone from his dark eyes. His words and the sound of his deep voice touched something in her memory, making her heart jump. His eyes caressed her flushed face.

"We could have talked on the phone. But all you did was shout at me." Her lower lip quivered as she remembered.

"I know, and I'm sorry about losing my temper. My only excuse is that I was worried. I guess I can also blame it on the fact that I haven't had anyone to share my anxieties with for so long, I find it hard to do." After a pause, he said quietly, "Marla and Crissy are going to try and take Mac-Dougle away from me. It would be their way to snatch him and work out the legal tangles later."

"No!" She stared at him in alarm. "Why? Why do they want him now? They didn't want him when he was so little, and so . . . weak and needed his mother's milk so desperately!"

"Money and status are the important things to them. Marla's family never approved of me. I got along with the old man all right, but his sons think I'm crude, uncultured — a barbarian!" he said with an amused laugh.

"If you didn't want me to leave Johnny here alone with a sitter and go to the dance class, why didn't you say so? What if someone had come while I was gone? Joy would have been frightened to death!"

"I didn't tell you because I knew you'd be worried. I put a round-the-clock watch on the house. You were followed even when you went to the grocery store, and I called the agency every day. I was reasonably sure you and MacDougle were safe for the time being, or I'd have been back. I wanted to get some business matters and this thing with Marla cleared up so when I came home I wouldn't have to leave again."

"I can't believe this! Why do they want him now when they didn't want him a few months ago? What are you going to do? Can they take him away from us?" Gaye was so upset she didn't realize she had used the word "us."

"They're going to try, sweetheart. I met with Marla's brothers in New York. Someone has shown up who claims to be Mac-Dougle's father, someone whose family hasn't produced an heir for a good long while. It's very important to some of the European families that their lineage continue. It seems there's a chance for a good marriage for Crissy — money and title not excluded," he added bitterly. "I went to France to talk to Marla and reason with her, but she and Crissy were off skiing in the Alps, and knowing I'd be madder than hell, they made sure I couldn't find them."

"Was that the reason you went to Europe?" She hoped that it was. She didn't want to think he had taken a holiday with Jean.

"Yes and . . . no. I sold six head of registered Appaloosa horses that Jean and I owned together to a breeder in southern France. A part of the deal — and this wasn't sprung on me until later — was that I'd fit them with a special type of shoe for that terrain. Another thing that was sprung on me at the last minute was the fact Jean was going along. I'm also selling a farm I have near Bowling Green that joins one Jean owns. I don't plan to retire. I'll still have my fingers in a few things, but I want to spend most of my time here with you and Mac-Dougle."

"Why did you let me think you were a blacksmith?" The bitterness she had felt for so many days seemed to dissolve in one shuddering sigh. All that remained was a tiredness and a doubt that she and this man could ever be totally compatible.

"I *am* a blacksmith, sweetheart. I love the work. I'm mapping out a course to teach at the college trade school this spring. It's a craft that helped to build America to what it is today. The West would never have been settled without the blacksmith. I'm also a mining engineer, investor, welder, writer, teacher, grandfather and I'm Irish to boot." He grinned.

"Be serious. I'm worried about Mac—about Johnny. To know he's with people who don't really love him, who're just using him for their own selfish reasons, would be more than I could endure!" She knew she was about to lose control. She clenched her jaws against the sobs that almost choked her.

"They're not going to take him away from you, Gaye. I told Marla's big-shot lawyer brothers that they'd get MacDougle over my dead body." A mischievous sparkle lighted his eyes. "They seemed to think that was a pretty good idea, especially after I slammed one of them into the wall."

"You didn't! They could have had you arrested, and how would that have looked at a trial!" She couldn't help but smile as the mental picture flashed through her mind.

"I need you, sweetheart. I need your calming influence. C'mere and let me hold you." He was stretched out on the recliner, his feet on the ottoman, his arms open.

It was tempting, but Gaye shook her head vigorously. There were too many unanswered questions. He seemed to read her mind.

"Tomorrow I'll take you and MacDougle out to my place. I want you to meet my mother and my aunt. I want you to know all there is to know about me. You already know that I'd rather be here with you than anywhere else in the world. I want you and need you like I never believed I'd want and need a woman. I'm not a young man, Gaye, but I'm financially secure if that's important to you. It's taken me a long time to find the woman I want to spend the rest of my life with. I'm not going to let you get away from me." He spoke so softly and so sincerely she could almost believe him. But there was still the hurt inside her.

"If what you say is true, why did you bring Jean here?" She looked at him in angry bewilderment.

He looked back at her calmly, and for a long while he didn't speak. Then, he said, "Anything I say will sound like a half-ass excuse. The truth is, and I didn't even know it at the time, I was crazy jealous when I saw you at the bar. You looked right through me, and my imagination soared, especially when I saw who you were with. Two of those women have quite a reputation around town. It hit me with the force of a freight train that you'd decided you wanted to play the field."

"But —"

He lifted a hand. "Let me tell you. I want you to know everything about me, and that includes my weaknesses. Jean is a beautiful woman, and when she insisted on seeing MacDougle, I brought her here. I was stroking my own ego. I wanted you to see that another woman thought I was desirable. It sounds like high-school stuff, doesn't it?" He raked his fingers through his hair. "Love makes people do stupid, unpredictable things. You'd think that a man my age would know better."

"I'm sorry you had so little faith in me." The words came out over the lump in her throat. "You could have called me and let me know you were in town."

"Jean met me at the airport. She'd taken an earlier flight from New York. She told me she had spoken to one of Marla's brothers and he'd revealed some new developments in Marla's plans to regain custody of MacDougle. Jean said she had made reservations and would tell me about it over dinner. I shouldn't have believed her, but I did. Her information didn't amount to a hill of beans!"

"I thought she lived in Bowling Green."

"She does. Her folks live here. Jean married into money, but ever since her husband died her main goal in life has been to marry me. Jean enjoys the chase. I got her interested in the horses, hoping she would find someone else. She's a snob at heart. But for some reason she thought she could polish me up and make me presentable." He laughed, a low chuckling sound. "I learned a long while ago, my darling, that I can be no less than what I am. I will bend if I honestly can, but I'll never change myself to someone else's specifications."

Gaye closed her eyes. She had to think! She had to sort out her emotions, untangle the confused motivations, and decide what she really wanted out of life. The endearment, the low, persuasive voice were wreaking havoc with her logic. She opened her eyes to see Jim leaving the chair. He bent and placed another log on the fire, replaced the screen. He straightened up, his eyes focused on her with an intense expression — loving, possessive, hungry and . . . wary.

"Marry me, Gaye. Marry me and we'll fight for MacDougle together." He sat down beside her. She held out her hand, palm up, as if to hold him away from her. He took it in his and moved it to his chest. She felt his heart leaping under it. The rest of him was still; a peculiar, silent waiting was between them.

"Can you possibly be thinking that I want you because of MacDougle? If you're thinking that, you're wrong. You underestimate yourself, sweetheart. I meant it when I told you that you're every sweet dream I've ever had rolled into one."

"Jim . . . don't be so nice to me. I can handle it much better when you . . . bellow and roar." Sudden tears ached behind her eyes.

"And I will again, sweetheart. I'm not a patient man. But . . . I've got a heart full of love for you."

Very softly she said, "Oh, Jim. I've been so miserable."

His eyes, soft with love, drank in her face. Then, with a deep sigh, he took her in his arms and held her close, her head resting on his shoulder, while he gently stroked her hair. They sat quietly, hugging each other, for a long while. Then he lifted her chin.

"I love you, babe. I love you. I never thought I'd ever say that." His voice was husky and quivered with emotion. Her words melted on her lips when she tried to speak, swept away by his kisses. "Hold me. I need you, my love." There was an anguish in his voice that pierced her heart.

"I . . . love you. Jim, I do love you!"

"Ahhhh . . . that's what I wanted to hear." He kissed her long and hard, his mouth taking savage possession of hers, parting her lips and invading them in a wild, sweet, wonderful way. His hands began to stroke her, moving everywhere, touching her hungrily from her thighs to her breasts. He leaned back and stretched out on the couch, taking her to lie on top of him. He positioned her thighs between his, pulled her up to lie on his chest and pressed her head to his shoulder. Her face found refuge against his neck. She felt his hands on her buttocks, pulling her tightly against him.

"Ahhhh . . ." he sighed. "This is the way it was the night before I left. I'm home. I'm really home."

He fell asleep almost immediately with his arms wrapped around her. She lay relaxed and contented on top of him. This moment was hers, and nothing could take this away from her. She listened to his steady breathing and watched the vein pulse in his throat. She burrowed her lips into the opening of his shirt, her nose into the fine black hair. He smelled male, with a faint overtone of soap and deodorant. She was suddenly conscious of the soft, vulnerable, male part of him nestled snugly against her upper thighs. A feeling of protectiveness for this big, rugged, lonely man washed over her, and she wanted to hold him to her breast and comfort him.

Feeling wonderfully happy and relaxed,

Gaye closed her eyes, thinking she would wait until he was sleeping soundly before she got up and went up to bed.

Then she, too, fell into a dreamless slumber.

Gaye became half awake and realized she was lying in bed and Jim's head lay on her breast. Fleeting memories of being carried up the stairs, of having her robe removed and being tucked into bed, flitted across her mind. She'd been so tired. She had opened her eyes one time and had seen Jim's face; then, feeling so loved and cared for, she had drifted back to sleep.

A sound penetrated her consciousness, and she came instantly awake. Johnny was crying. She glanced at the clock on the table. It's no wonder he's crying, she thought guiltily. It's almost an hour past his regular feeding time.

The weight of Jim's head on her breast was achingly sweet. Her arms curved about him tenderly. She had never felt so completely a woman as she hugged the shaggy head and pressed her lips to his forehead. This big, rough, self-assured man needed her!

She eased him out of her arms and tried to move away so she could get out of bed.

His arms reached for her and pulled her snugly against him. He curled around her like a contented kitten.

"Don't go," he whispered against the top of her head.

"I've got to. Johnny's crying for his bottle."

"He's had you all to himself for weeks. It's my turn," he grumbled sleepily.

Gaye laughed softly against his hairy chest. "You big baby. You've got to learn to share."

"Well . . . all right. But kiss me first and . . . come right back." His words were husky and love-slurred.

She lifted her lips, his mouth taking hers in a kiss that engaged her soul. His lips hardened, and her own parted under them, admitting him, submitting. She touched the tip of her tongue delicately against his mouth and felt him tremble, felt his body stir against her stomach. His hands moved to her buttocks to press her against him.

"Jim. . . . we can't. . . ." Her muttered words were barely coherent.

He loosened his arms and she rolled away. "Bring him in here." His voice reached her at the door.

Johnny was wet, hungry and angry. Gaye changed his diaper, put him in a dry sleeper and carried him downstairs. He was somewhat happier by the time the bottle came from the microwave, and sucked on it lustily as she carried him back up the stairs to her bedroom.

Jim lifted the covers, and she lay down beside him holding the infant in her arms. Her head rested on Jim's arm, and he pulled her tightly into the curve of his body. He lifted his head and his lips nuzzled her cheek. His hand cupped his grandson's bottom and he shook him gently. The baby smiled around the nipple in his mouth.

"You little imp! You're not playing fair." He placed kisses along Gaye's jawline and whispered in her ear. "You went downstairs without your slippers. Your feet are like ice cubes. No . . . don't move them away." He lifted a warm bare leg over hers and pressed her feet to him with the bottom of his. "Your feet wouldn't be this cold if you were still breast-feeding him," he murmured.

"Oh, Jim. Do you think they'll take him away from us?" She turned her head so she could whisper against his mouth.

"We'll do everything we can to see that he stays right here where he belongs."

"Your daughter signed away her rights to him. She doesn't deserve to have him."

"My lawyer says they'll probably say she signed under duress, that I pressured her into signing him over to me. But don't worry about it now, sweetheart."

"I can't help worrying. He's ours!" Her arms tightened about the infant.

"We'll build the best case we can to keep him legally without digging up dirt. But if we think there's a chance we'll lose him, I'll pull out all the stops. I know things about Marla and my daughter that the *National Enquirer* would love to know, and I'll spill everything before I'll give him up to them."

Gaye was shocked at the viciousness in his voice. "Good heavens! Do you think it'll come to that?"

"It could. Marla sees a chance to get a titled husband for Crissy. We're going to have to get our house in order, sweetheart. And that means getting married right away. I'd planned to wait and give you a chance to get adjusted to the idea. It isn't a quick decision on my part. I hope you know that. I've wanted you since that first day when I came into the hospital room and saw you nursing MacDougle," he said huskily, and his hand burrowed between her and the baby to cup around her breast. "Are you going to nurse all our kids?"

"I suppose so." Her lips desperately sought his. After the long, deep kiss, she whispered, "Oh, Jim! It's like a wonderful dream with a nightmare hovering over it."

"MacDougle's asleep, sweetheart. I'll put him back in the crib so I can have you all to myself." Jim kissed the bare warm curve of her neck, following it to her ear and back to the hollow in her shoulder, covering her skin with light, tantalizing kisses.

"Turn him over on his tummy and cover him." She ran the tip of her tongue around the velvety inside of her lips as his had done, and her heart leaped in anticipation.

Jim lifted the infant from her arms and held him against his bare chest. His dark eyes moved from his grandson to Gaye's face. His smile was beautiful.

"I'm a fool to be so happy. But I'd given up on meeting a woman like you and having a family of my own."

"No more of a fool than I am." She was thrilled by the deep, velvety look absorbing her and held out her arms. "Put the baby down, love, and come back to me. The next hour or so is mine."

When he returned Gaye had time for only one thought: He's handsome with his clothes on, but naked he's magnificent! Jim slipped into bed beside her and without any hesitancy claimed her lips in a fierce kiss. She opened her mouth and honored his ownership. Her heart beat with pure joy. He was forging chains that were binding him to her forever.

"Sweetheart, you're so beautiful. How have I survived this long without you? I love the feel of your breasts and the taste of your mouth. You're so soft, so feminine, so incredibly sweet!" His words were groaned thickly into her ear.

The deeply buried heat in her body flared out of control, and she sought his mouth hungrily. Her hands moved to his back, digging into the smooth muscles. He stroked her, whispering words, their meaning muffled as he kissed her soft, rounded breasts, nibbled with his teeth, nuzzled with his lips. He was totally absorbed in giving her pleasure and at the same time pleasing himself.

"Jim . . ."

"Hmmm?"

"Jim, darling —"

His hands cupped her hips and lifted her to him. "Do you really want to talk, love?" he asked an instant before his mouth settled over hers and the tip of his tongue found welcome inside her lips.

She couldn't have talked then if she had wanted to. Besides, she had forgotten what she was going to say.

■ ■ ■ ■

Gaye cooked breakfast while Jim showered. He came down to the kitchen carrying his grandson in the crook of his arm. His black hair was wet and glistening. It seemed strange to Gaye to see him in her kitchen wearing the trousers to his dark suit and his wrinkled white shirt, opened at the neck and the sleeves rolled up to his elbows.

"I changed his pants. Phew! How long until he uses the bathroom like civilized folk?"

Gaye laughed happily. "A couple of years, at least." She lifted bacon out to drain on a paper towel. "How many eggs?"

"Three or four . . . and toast. I'm hungry as a bear."

"And you look like one, too." She let her fingertips drag across the stubble on his cheek. He grabbed her hand and brought it to his lips.

"I'll have to start shaving morning and night." He flashed her a wide, happy smile. "I don't want my whiskers to scratch your soft skin." He cupped the back of her head with one hand and kissed her soundly.

Gaye's arms went around him. The infant squirmed between them. This was more than she'd ever hoped to have. She leaned into his kiss, and when he released her she looked up at him with eyes shining with love.

"I'll gladly have my face scratched for that," she whispered.

While they were eating breakfast, Jim told her about his mother.

"She's the fourth generation to live on the farm. She and her sister have lived there together since my father was killed in the Pacific during the war. I went to school on my father's insurance money, roamed around a bit, married and decided the fast lane wasn't the life for me. I came back to the farm and have been there ever since, except for occasional business trips."

"Will we live there?" It was the first time the question of where they would live had crossed her mind.

"We'll live wherever you want to live. If you want to live here in your house, it's okay by me. If you want to live out at the farm, I'll build you a house. My mother is in the advanced stage of diabetes. She's very frail and almost blind. After my mother is gone, my aunt will stay in the home place for as long as she lives."

"Are you an only child?" Gaye asked quietly.

"Yes. I was born after my father went to war. It was lonely being raised without a father or brothers and sisters. We'll see that it doesn't happen to MacDougle." His eyes held hers, and her heart thudded painfully at the tenderness she saw there.

"Did Crissy stay with your mother while she was here?"

"No. I wouldn't subject my mother and aunt to her rudeness. I had a mobile home moved in for her to live in." His voice was quiet and solid as steel, and Gaye wished she hadn't asked the question.

"Is that where Johnny and I would have lived if I'd come out to the farm to take care of him?"

"Yes. I thought you'd rather have a place of your own. But since you didn't come, I had it hauled out."

"I'm sorry about your mother's illness."

"All I can do for her now is to see to it that she's as comfortable as possible and that she stays in her home. That's what she wants to do. I wanted to take you out to see her before I left, but I wasn't sure how you'd react. It's not a glamorous place by any means, but it's my home and I love it and I hope you'll love it too," he said tersely, his face dark and taut with feeling, his eyes the smoldering black she knew so well.

She covered the back of his hand with her palm, and his turned to clasp tightly about her fingers.

"How could I not love something you love so much? It doesn't matter to me where we live as long as I'm with you."

"Thanks, sweetheart. You like this house. You feel at home here and so do I. We can live here until we decide what we want to do. We may want to build a new house on the farm, or remodel the old one for our large family." The endearing grin that made him look years younger spread over his face. "Shall we stay here today and start work on that project? I'm not getting any younger, you know."

"We worked on that this morning, Mr. Trumbull." Gaye got up from the table and gave a strand of his hair a little jerk when she passed him. He grabbed her arm and pulled her around and down on his lap. His lips nuzzled her neck.

"You tease! You make me want you so, I can't keep my hands off you."

Gaye wound her arms about his neck and hugged him fiercely. Her hands moved across the muscles of his back and up to grasp his hair, pulling the tip of his nose against hers. "Our boy needs his food," she said in a loud whisper.

Jim looked over her shoulder at the infant. "Young man," he said sternly, "we're going to have to come to an understanding about this woman. I'll share her during the day, but at night she's all mine."

CHAPTER ELEVEN

Gaye sat beside Jim in the big sedan. He had removed the padded car seat from her Buick and installed it in the backseat of his car for his grandson. The morning had flown by almost as fast as the landscape was flying past now.

"What will your mother think about all this? Will she be surprised?"

"She'll be pleased. I've told her about you." His long fingers burrowed down between her thighs and pulled the one next to his tightly against him. "But even if she wasn't, she wouldn't say anything. She taught me to be my own person, just as she is."

Gaye sat back in the seat and drew a deep breath. Tomorrow she would be married to this man. She hadn't even had the chance to tell Alberta and Lila yet about the marriage ceremony that would take place at the Methodist church.

Twenty-four hours ago she had been miserable and had thought she would never be happy again. Now her life had taken on a new radiance. It seemed so right to be sitting here beside Jim with Johnny strapped safely in the seat behind them.

She started when she heard Jim's voice. "What's the matter, sweetheart? Are you worried about meeting my mother and aunt and seeing my home?"

"No. I'm not worried about anything. That's what bothers me. Everything seems so right for me. It's as if this had been planned out in advance. The only thing that keeps me from being supremely happy is the threat of losing Johnny."

"Don't worry about that now. Let's take things one step at a time. Marla asked me to give him back to them; I said no. The next step is up to them. My former in-laws are very mercenery, yet very proud. They would hate to have this dragged through a court of law and all the dirty linen aired. That's a big plus in our favor."

Jim braked sharply as they rounded a curve and waited patiently for the rural-mail carrier to pull off the road. The grass that filled the ditches on each side of the road and grew along the fence line was now dried by the frosts. They passed through a heavily wooded area, the leafless branches of the trees stark against the sky, and came to the flat farm country. Occasionally they passed a farm where the huge barn dwarfed the house, a one-lane track connecting it to the road. The pastures were marked off with a network of white board fence, a small number of horses in each enclosure. At one farm a beautiful black horse, its lead rope attached to the circular exercise machine, trotted majestically with his head and his tail high.

They talked off and on, but impersonally, about the land, wild animals and birds. Jim was a conservationist, and part of his land was a game preserve. He was vehemently opposed to indiscriminate hunters. He was especially vocal about hunting with a bow and arrow.

"I've found several deer that had crawled off to die with an arrow stuck in them. About a month ago I came on a horned owl that had been killed. I sent it to the state conservation commission, where it'll be preserved and shown to schoolchildren. Sad as it is, someday that may be the only way they'll see one."

He told her about the horse farm he had over near Paducah and the breeding program for his registered Appaloosa horses.

He explained his reason for selling the farm at Bowling Green.

"The offer was just too good to turn down," he said with a grin.

The road bent to the left. Jim turned abruptly to the right and onto a narrow drive. A metal gate barred their way, and he got out to open it. The drive was smooth and covered with fine gravel. Evergreen trees crowded the lane as it wound back into the hills. As the trees began to thin, Gaye caught a glimpse of the farmhouse. From a distance it looked small. As they drew near she could see it was made of native stone. The front part of the house was two storied, the back part a single story with a side porch attached. A long board porch with a single step and a sloping roof ran across the front of the house, with two front doors opening onto it, and continued along the side. There were several barns and sheds and a newer building that sat off to the side in a grove of trees.

Jim stopped the car in front of another gate. A picket fence enclosed the home area. Gaye immediately thought of the song "Old MacDonald had a Farm." A big shepherd dog barked a greeting; ducks and geese waddled about the yard. Big fluffy chickens, both red and white, cackled and strutted.

Two sheep looked them over indifferently and went on eating grass. Just when Gaye thought she had seen it all, her startled eyes found a billy goat perched on top of a pile of neatly cut wood.

After Jim closed the gate behind them, he got into the car and sat looking at her. Finally he spoke. "I have to put the car in the garage." He jerked his head toward the woodpile. "Ralph will lose no time climbing on top of it if I leave it out. He can cut up a vinyl top in no time at all." He searched her face. "You're so quiet. Does it overwhelm you?"

"I was just thinking of what a wonderful place this would be to bring a second-grade class. Some of the children I've taught have never been on a farm or seen animals outside a zoo."

Jim laughed. "What you see is only the tip of the iceberg. I've got cows, horses, a raccoon running around that refuses to leave, a couple of burros and a donkey named Hortense. About the only thing you won't find here is pigs. Someone gave me a runt to raise when I was a boy. We couldn't butcher it after I became attached to it. It grew to about seven hundred pounds and died of old age. He'd probably eaten seven hundred dollars worth of corn during his lifetime."

Gaye watched his face. He seemed to be relieved. Was he afraid I'd be disappointed? she wondered. She had to admit it was a little more than she'd expected. But now that she saw him in these surroundings she could see why he'd never be happy with a woman like Jean Wisner.

They drove to a garage behind the barn. The door raised as they approached the building. Jim drove inside and the door came down. He pulled in alongside his black pickup truck.

"This garage is the only building on the place that's animal- and bird-proof. I don't care much about driving to town and finding I've brought along a chicken or a cat." He turned off the motor, swung an arm up over her head and gripped her shoulder, pulling her to him. "I want to kiss you. I've been thinking about it all the way from town." His voice lowered huskily as his lips came close to hers.

"Then get on with it, love. I've been waiting, too." Her eyes danced lovingly over his face, and her hand inched up to curl about his neck.

The kiss was long and deep and full of promised passion that flared whenever they touched. His fingers moved up into her hair, their touch strong and possessive. She took his kiss thirstily. She wanted to stay there forever. His lips pulled away, but he drew her closely to him.

"I love you," he said quietly.

"I love you, too. I want to be with you forever."

"You shall be. My life has been empty up to now. You fill it completely." He kissed her again. Her lips were clinging moistly to his. His hand slipped inside her coat and up under her sweater. His eyes held hers while his fingers cupped about the flesh held in the lacy cup. Her nipple hardened, and drops of milk moistened her bra. "You still have milk," he whispered huskily.

"A little."

His lips fell hungrily to hers. They were demanding, yet tender. His tongue deeply invaded the mouth that parted so eagerly and grazed over pearl white teeth.

"We'd better stop this or I won't be able to go into the house for a while."

She laughed and pulled away from him. "We're like a couple of teenagers making out in a parked car. C'mon. Your mother and aunt will wonder what we're doing."

Jim carried the baby and Gaye walked beside him. Ducks and chickens were waiting when they came out of the building. Jim threw out a handful of grain he took from the barrel inside the garage door. A big white duck pecked at the shiny end of Gaye's shoelace, and she jumped back.

"You have to watch out for Kathryn," Jim said. "She gets pretty aggressive and can hurt you. She'll make a grab for anything that looks good to eat." Kathryn quacked, fluffed her feathers and strutted ahead of them.

"Do they all have names?"

"Most of them. We have two pet crows, so don't be frightened if one of them swoops down and lands on your shoulder. They like shiny, pretty things, too." He smiled down at her. "I took off my watch one day, and the minute I laid it down one of them grabbed it and flew up in a tree and hid it. I had a heck of a time shimmying up that tree to get it. Sometimes they'll meet the truck at the end of the lane and fly beside me all the way to the house."

"This is a wonderful place for children. It's no wonder you wanted your grandson with you."

They went up onto the porch that ran along the side of the house. The door opened as if someone had been watching and waiting. Jim stood back so she could enter.

Her first impression was that she had stepped back fifty years. The kitchen was warm, cozy and neat as a pin. A big black cookstove and an upright kitchen cabinet sat side by side. Shelves curtained with checked gingham lined the walls. In the middle of the room a round oak table and high-backed chairs sat on an oval braided rug. A potted African violet sat in the center of the cloth-covered table.

The woman who stood beside the door was elderly. She was small and neat and held herself erect. Her dress came within six inches of the floor and was covered with a bibbed apron. Soft gray hair was smoothed back and twisted in a bun at the nape of her neck. Her eyes were dark and met Gaye's warily. Gaye was thankful for Jim's big bulk that crowded into the doorway behind her.

"Hello, Aunt Minnie. This is Gaye."

"Hello." Gaye held out her hand. The woman hesitated and then took it for an instant in hers. Her eyes swung to Jim's, then down to the infant in his arms, and a smile faintly lifted the corners of her mouth.

"Hold him, Aunt Minnie, while I help Gaye with her coat." Jim placed Johnny in her arms. She held him carefully and moved away. "I forgot to tell you that Aunt Minnie doesn't speak," he whispered in her ear. He took her coat, hung it on a wooden peg beside the door and hung his beside it.

"We should take him out of the bunting bag," Gaye said gently. The woman lifted her gaze from the baby to Gaye. Gaye smiled and reached for the strings to untie the hood, then pulled down the zipper. "So you decided to wake up, did you?" she said to the wide-eyed child and lifted him out of the bag. She waited for the silent woman to place it on the back of a chair and handed Johnny back to her, praying he wouldn't cry as he had done the night Jean took him. He didn't. Gaye gave a sigh of relief and looked about.

Now she could see some modern equipment tucked away out of sight — an electric stove, a refrigerator-freezer, a washer-dryer. She caught a glimpse of a dishwasher adorned with a crocheted scarf and another potted African violet. I'll bet it's never used, she thought with a smile.

"We'd better take them in to see Mama, Aunt Minnie. She'll accuse us of plotting against her," Jim said teasingly and put his arm across the thin shoulders and gave her a hug. "Aunt Minnie has been a big part of my life," he said to Gaye. "I can't remember a time when she wasn't here for me to come to."

It was clear to Gaye, Jim's aunt adored him. She looked like a tiny sparrow standing next to him. She smiled up into his face, her eyes flashing a message only the two of them understood.

Jim enfolded Gaye's hand in his, and they followed the slim, erect figure through a dining room and into a living room, where a narrow stairway divided the front rooms and led to the rooms above. She led them into a large room. Jim's mother lay in a high hospital bed beside a large plate-glass window. She appeared to be a fleshier version of her sister.

"Hello, Mama. I brought Gaye and MacDougle to see you."

"Good. Bring her over so I can get a look at her."

Jim pulled Gaye toward the bed. Gaye remembered him telling her his mother was almost blind, and she wondered how much she could see.

"Hello, Mrs. Trumbull."

"Hello, lass. Sit down so I can see your face. Jim says you're not silly pretty." Gaye sat down and leaned forward. The gray head lifted, the clouded dark eyes narrowed and strained. "You'll do." She let her head fall back. "I like her face, son. Does she have any gumption to go with it?"

Gaye's startled eyes sought Jim's — his were twinkling. He towered above them, and she had to tilt her head far back to see his face. At this moment he reminded her of the Jolly Green Giant. His hand gripped her shoulder, and she returned his smile.

"Yes, Mama. She's not only got horse sense, she's got good teeth. Show her, honey." Gaye pinched him on the leg. He squeezed her shoulder in retaliation. "We're going to be married tomorrow. She knows a good thing when she sees one."

"I figured she was the one you wanted. It's time you took a wife. This'n got to be an improvement over the other'n." There was a touch of humor in her voice.

Jim's laugh was loud and boisterous. "She is. I waited a long time to find her. She's a lot like you, Mama. She's sassy and independent, but smart as a whip and has all the mating instincts. I'll be able to manage her if I keep her pregnant."

Mrs. Trumbull chuckled and Gaye's jaw dropped in amazement.

"I'd like to see that, son. You'll just have to tell me about it. Are you going to say anything, girl?"

"How can I?" Gaye sputtered. "You two

seem to have things figured out."

"You've got grit, lass. You'll need it with my Jim."

"It seems I'll need a strong back, too."

Mrs. Trumbull laughed again, and Gaye wondered how she could be so cheerful. She got up from the chair when Jim urged his aunt toward the bed.

"MacDougle is growing by leaps and bounds, Mama."

"Lay him here beside me, son. Oh, my! You had hair like this when you were a baby. Didn't he, Minnie?"

Gaye stood back and watched. There seemed to be no lack of communication between the sisters. Johnny kicked, blew spit and enjoyed the attention he was getting. Jim hovered over them for a moment, then backed away to stand beside Gaye. His arm came around her and she looked up. The sad expression on his face touched her deeply, and her eyes misted over.

"Aunt Minnie, do you suppose you and Mama can manage MacDougle for a little while? I want to take Gaye out to my workshop."

The gray head nodded eagerly, and Jim urged Gaye to the door with his hand in the small of her back.

The minute they stepped out the door,

the big white duck ran to greet them, fluffing her feathers and quacking.

"Nothing this time, Kathryn. Run along, you're getting too fat. You'll find yourself in someone's pot if you're not careful." Jim spoke in a conversational tone, as if the duck understood every word he said, which she must have done because she turned and walked haughtily away. "Begone with you, too, Ralph," he said to the goat that walked up behind them and tried to get in between them. "You'll have to wait until Gaye gets acquainted with you before you get familiar."

"Oh, Jim," Gaye said and laughed, her eyes shining as she looked up into his. "This is a wonderful place."

"I'm glad you think so, sweetheart," he said, and his arm hugged her to him. "I want to show you my iron sculptures."

He led her down a dirt path toward a low building set among the trees. Nestled among the grasses along the path and backed against bushes and trees were an assortment of animal figures made of iron and painted in dull earthy colors. A deer, its head held in an alert position, stood partially hidden among the lilac bushes. In the grasses were rabbits, and attached to a tree trunk was a saucy squirrel. There was a skunk trailed by little ones, a fox, a turkey with its tail feathers spread, lambs, cows, goats, all life-size.

"I can't believe this." Gaye's laugh rang on the crisp, cool air. "I love the way you've placed them in their natural surroundings. They're *good,* Jim."

"I don't know how good they are, but it's something that gives me pleasure to do." His dark eyes ravished her face, bright with happiness.

"People should see them," she said enthusiastically. "You should share your talent. Have you sold any of them?"

"One or two." He shrugged. "C'mon. I want to show you what I'm working on now." With his arm about her he led her into the building. A half-finished figure of a horse stood braced against a framework. Jim handed her a glossy picture. "This is Falcon Grey, the stallion that started me in the breeding business. Someday he'll stand beside the gate to the farm."

"He's beautiful," Gaye murmured, but her mind was saying, How could I have fallen in love with a man I knew so little about? She looked into his craggy face and her eyes mirrored the love in her heart. "So are you," she whispered.

"If you look at me like that, sweetheart, I'll —"

She moved close to him, delighting him by snuggling in his arms. "You'll what?" she murmured and held her lips up for his kiss.

He kissed her quickly. "I'll forget that it's cold in here, and that MacDougle may be squalling by now, and ravish you."

"I'm tempted," she said against his lips before she pulled away from him. "Is this where you do the horseshoeing?"

"Sometimes. But I have a mobile unit in the truck, too."

"You're a man of many facets, Mr. Trumbull."

"Sure I am." His eyes teased her. "I'm sweet, adorable, kind, overly intelligent, and patient."

"All true except for the last one, and I suspect your grandson doesn't have much either. We'd better get back to the house."

Later, when they were in the car going back to town, she asked him why his mother wasn't in a hospital or a nursing home.

"It's her choice," he said simply. "She wants to be home even if it means she won't live as long. A nurse comes each morning, and the doctor visits once a week."

"But in case of an emergency what would they do? Your aunt couldn't call for help."

"They don't feel Aunt Minnie has a

handicap at all. She's been that way since birth. I've made a tape recording. All she has to do is dial the number and turn on the machine. They're not out there alone. I have a man who lives on the place and looks after the animals. Even when I'm there I spend most of my time in the shop."

"We should come here more often. I feel so selfish now about not wanting to come out to the farm to take care of Johnny. All the time you've spent with me, you should've spent with them."

"I don't crowd them, sweetheart. They would resent it if I hovered over them. They're both proud and independent women. They live the way they want to live."

"Like you, darling. Oh, Jim! I love you so much."

Large, fluffy snowflakes fell on Gaye's wedding day, covering the ground like a blanket and making everything sparkling white and clean. Lila and the two preschool children she took care of during the day came to stay with Johnny while they went to the church for the ceremony. Alberta and her two teenagers and Candy, the nurse from the hospital, had been invited to the ceremony and would come to the house later in the evening for a small wedding reception. Lila and her children were also invited. As long as it was impossible for Jim's mother and aunt to attend the wedding, Jim arranged to have the ceremony filmed and recorded to play back for them later.

Gaye wore a soft blue cashmere suit she had worn only a few times before. She wore her snow boots and carried slender high-heeled pumps in her hand.

"Is this your only coat?" Jim asked as he helped her into a hooded parka.

"It's the only one suitable for this kind of weather."

"We'll remedy that," he promised and slipped into a dark overcoat. He had made a trip to the farm and returned with several boxes and suitcases of his personal things.

On the way to the church he stopped at the florist for a bouquet of white roses for Gaye and a boutonniere for himself. Jim had said he would take care of everything and he had. He even ordered a wedding cake to be delivered to the house while they were away.

In the church foyer Jim dusted the snow flakes from his dark, shaggy head and hung their coats on the hooks in the alcove provided. They stood for a moment in the back of the almost-empty church, Gaye's trembling hand clasped firmly in his. Alberta, Brett and Joy sat in the first pew and Candy sat behind them. The minister came out to stand at the end of the aisle, and the guests stood and faced the back of the church.

Slowly and solemnly, their fingers entwined in a knot of love, Jim and Gaye came forward and took their places to say their vows. The ceremony itself was simple. The minister, a portly man with wisps of gray hair combed over his almost-bald head, spoke his words in a hushed, reverent tone.

It was not a fairy-tale wedding. There was no music and there were no banks of flowers for them to stand before. Gaye was not a virgin Cinderella. Jim was no Prince Charming. It was basic and *real.* Today she was joining her life to that of a rugged, earthy man who would love, cherish and protect her and their children. They would live out the days of their lives together, grow old together. She wouldn't wake up again to a day of loneliness stretching out before her.

"Do you, James, take this woman . . . in sickness and in health . . . to love and to cherish . . . ?"

The voice brought her back to the present, and her eyes went quickly to Jim's and found that he was looking down at her.

"I do." He spoke only to her.

"Do you, Gaye, take this man . . . ?"

At the proper time Jim slipped a narrow gold band on her finger. She was scarcely aware of it. His dark, serious eyes held hers until the ceremony was over. He bent down and brushed her trembling lips with his, and interlaced his fingers with hers.

"Congratulations, Jim. Welcome to the family." Alberta kissed his cheek. Joy and Brett shook his hand while Alberta folded her sister in her arms. "I'm so happy for you, Gaye," she whispered, her eyes bright with tears. "You and Jim will have a good life together."

"Oh, Aunt Gaye, I thought it a shame there weren't going to be many people here, but it was so private, so special. This is just the kind of wedding I want." Joy looked up at Jim. "Do I call you 'uncle' now?"

"Of course," Jim said, and everyone laughed.

After the guests left the foyer, Jim and Gaye followed the minister to his office and signed their names to the marriage certificate. Jim put his name beneath hers with bold strokes of the pen. He took some bills from his wallet. The minister shook his head.

"A donation for the Sunday school," Jim

insisted. "You can expect a horde of new students in a few years."

The minister glanced at Gaye's suddenly flushed face and accepted the bills. "Well, in that case — thank you."

Alone in the church foyer, Jim took her in his arms and kissed her tenderly and reverently.

"Hello, there, Mrs. James M. Trumbull," he whispered between kisses.

"What's the M. for?"

"Guess."

"MacDougle?"

"What else?" He chuckled, and she could feel the movement against her breasts.

"It was a beautiful ceremony," Gaye said, her eyes moist.

"You're a beautiful bride."

"I *do* love you."

"Keep saying it, sweetheart. It makes me want to move mountains for you."

"I don't want you to do anything as dramatic as that. I just want you with me for the rest of my life."

"I wish we'd met when we were younger. We've wasted so much time."

"Don't waste time wishing for what might have been. We may not have been suited for each other then."

"I doubt that," he said strongly, his dark

eyes glowing warmly. "But let's go home and argue about it . . . in bed."

Gaye felt a sudden, delicious rush of joy. She was utterly in love with this man, the real man behind the rough exterior. She laughed aloud at the thought of what Kathy, the woman from the dance class, would say about her marrying the caveman. Caveman? With her he was a gentle pussycat. She suspected she saw a side of him he never showed to anyone else.

"What are you laughing about?" Jim helped her into her coat.

"I was wondering if you were going to throw me over your shoulder and carry me off to your cave?"

"Why would you be wondering a thing like that?"

"Never mind. I'll tell you tonight . . . in bed."

Gaye sat close beside him in the car, her hand curled possessively beneath his inner thigh. The warm light in his eyes and the smile on his face told her more than any words that this was a special day in his life. He stopped at the liquor store for a bottle of champagne, and she waited patiently, her eyes glued to the door where he would come out. Full realization had not yet soaked in that he was hers, exclusively hers.

Jim returned to the car and they kissed. Gaye touched the smile creases near his mouth and fingered the thick dark brows. They lingered in the snow-covered car. She wanted to touch him everywhere. The intimacy they shared was heady. Her hand moved along his thigh until he captured it in his.

"You sure put a strain on this old man's control," he said huskily. "We'd better go home."

They drove slowly. It began to snow in earnest. Huge, fluffy flakes splattered against the windshield. Gaye rested her cheek against the side of his arm and looked up at him with laughing eyes.

"I'm sure Lila won't stay long," she murmured.

"If she stays a minute, it'll be too long," he said and leered at her lustily. "I'm going to attack you the instant she's out the door."

"Cross your heart and hope to die?" she said in a singsong voice.

"Poke a needle in my eye." He mimicked her tone.

Their laughter rang deep and joyous.

Jim pulled into the drive and braked behind Lila's station wagon. Gaye gathered up her roses and got out of the car. Lila was standing just outside the door. From the expression on her face, Gaye knew immediately something was terribly wrong. Her heartbeat paused, then began a mad gallop.

"What is it? Lila! What's wrong."

"Two men and a woman came. They took the baby!"

Her shocking words knocked Gaye right off her cloud. The magic had ended.

CHAPTER TWELVE

"Sonofabitch!" Jim pushed Gaye ahead of him through the open door. "Did you call the police? Why in the hell didn't you," he roared when Lila shook her head.

"They had papers, a court order. One of the men said you had taken Gaye away so the parting wouldn't be so painful. The woman went upstairs and got Johnny."

"When? What did they look like? What kind of car were they driving?" Jim fired questions at Lila. His facial muscles were stretched taut with a terrible tension.

"Right after you left." Lila twisted her hands together in anguish. "I think they came in a cream-colored car with a brown top."

"What did they say?"

"They said they had a court order. They showed me the papers. I don't know about such things, but they looked official. The man was so self-assured. He . . ."

"Was the woman tall? Did she have black hair?"

"Yes. She had black hair and thin eyebrows. She was wearing a fur coat and high-heeled boots. One of the men was thin and had black hair with gray on the sides. The other man was heavyset and didn't say anything. I'm sorry, Gaye. Oh, God, I'm so sorry. I opened the door, and before I knew it they had pushed their way in. I didn't know what to do!"

"Marla and those damn brothers of hers!" Jim's angry voice filled every corner of the house.

If Gaye hadn't been so numb she would have trembled at his rage. Instead she stood motionless. She had a strange emptiness inside. The feeling was familiar, and after a moment she identified it. She'd felt this way after her baby died. No wonder she felt the same, because there'd been another sudden death. The death of happiness. She wondered vaguely when the numbness would wear off, and grief tear at her.

Lila's young charges sat quietly on the couch — two small bewildered creatures watching the big angry man.

"Did they take his formula?" Gaye spoke in a calm voice, as if they were discussing the weather.

"No. The woman came down with Johnny wrapped in a blanket and they left. They didn't take anything, or ask for his bottles."

"They don't know what to feed him. He'll be sick!" The sense of a waking nightmare dropped from Gaye. This was real!

"They had someone watching the house," Jim snarled. "They knew we'd left Mac-Dougle here. Damn!" He shrugged out of his overcoat and went to the telephone. He talked to someone at the airport. "I want to know every charter that has come in and gone out in the last three or four hours. Yes, some bastards have snatched my grandson. I know who it is! To hell with the police! I've got to stop them before they take him out of the country. Thanks, Tom. I'll be out there as soon as I can."

Jim called another number and talked to his attorney. When he finished he took the stairs two at a time and minutes later came back down the same way. He was wearing jeans, a sweater and boots. His hair was wild, his slanting eyes gleamed darkly, his jaw set at a brutal angle. He was in a dangerous mood.

"C'mon, Gaye. We're going to get our son back and crack a few heads while we're doing it." Gaye's eyes were full of misery when they looked up at him. He put his hands on her shoulders and gave her a gentle shake. "Now isn't the time to lose confidence in your old man. We'll get him back if we have to go all the way to France." He opened the closet door and snatched a stocking cap from the shelf, put it on her head and pulled it down over her ears. He turned to Lila. "I'm sorry I was so abrupt. You couldn't have stopped them." He took Gaye's hand and pulled her to the door.

"Wait!" She broke away, ran up the stairs to the baby's room and threw some things in the diaper bag. Downstairs, she added a couple of bottles of formula from the refrigerator and returned to Jim. "He'll be wet and hungry."

"Good thinking."

"I'll lock the house and go on home. Shall I call your sister?" Lila's face was still pale and her voice quivered nervously.

"Yes, please." Gaye went to her and hugged her briefly. "We don't blame you, Lila. Please don't feel bad."

"You'll call me?" Lila asked tearfully.

"As soon as we can."

Jim had cleaned the snow from the windshield by the time Gaye came out. He swung the car in a sharp turn and they were out the drive and on the street.

"I'm depending on this snow to keep the

planes grounded," he said and turned on the defroster as the inside windows began to steam up.

"How do you know they'll go by plane?"

"That's the only way they know to travel. When I called the airport they said a small Lear jet came in about noon and that the pilot was in there now trying to file a flight plan, but they doubted if the plane could take off because of the snow."

"It may not be them."

"They arrived in that plane, and they may try to leave in it. But they may have a larger plane coming in that could fly in this weather." He swore viciously. "If she weren't a woman I'd break her neck!" he snarled and rolled down the window to rid it of clinging snow so he could see before he crossed an intersection.

"How far is the . . . airport?" A sob tore from her throat and Gaye closed her eyes against the thought of not ever seeing Johnny again.

"Don't fall apart on me, honey." Jim's hand worked its way beneath her skirt to cup the inside of her nylon-clad knee. "You should have worn slacks. You're trembling."

"I'm not cold, I'm scared." Her chin quivered slightly and her voice was trembly.

"It was stupid of me not to think they'd

have someone here keeping an eye on us, sweetheart. Someone probably followed me to the florist last night and heard me say we were going to be married today. They notified Marla and she flew in this morning to wait her chance. When we catch up to them, I'm going to slap a kidnapping charge on them. I'm surprised those stupid brothers of hers took a chance like this. There must be a lot of money at stake."

"Will you really do that?" She had to keep talking or she would cry.

"You're damn right! They've screwed around with me long enough!"

She could hear the menace behind his angry words. He was like a combustible furnace ready to explode. I've got to be calm, she thought. The wrong word from me could be the spark that ignited the blaze in him. He's so angry he could kill someone!

They turned up the one-way drive leading to the low, flat terminal building. It was flanked on each side by steel hangars. There was a charter service and a flying school in the complex. The one commercial airliner that had stopped here, Jim explained, had canceled its run, and now the airport was serviced by two commuter-plane companies.

Jim stopped the car at the main entrance,

opened the door and got out. Gaye jumped out of the car and trailed him into the terminal lobby. His long legs ate up the distance from the door to the front desk. He threw back a folding counter and went into an office. He turned at the door.

"Stay here." He threw the words back over his shoulder, and Gaye halted in her tracks. She stood there, suddenly realizing that there was nothing she could do to calm him. It would be like pouring a cup of water on a roaring blaze.

Gaye remembered the diaper bag and ran back to the car to get it. It was getting dark. The wind pulled at her, whipping her face with snow and tugging at her skirt. There was no activity on the road or in the sparsely occupied parking lot. All around her there was only the approaching darkness and the curtain of driving snow.

Jim was coming out of the office when she returned to the lobby. He had another man with him, and the man was trying to reason with him.

"I know you're mad, Jim. I don't blame you. But don't do anything they could use against you. They're not going anywhere. The pilot is too smart to take off in this. We won't give him clearance. If he takes off without it and something happens to his plane, his insurance isn't worth a damn."

Gaye trailed behind them. They stopped at large double glass doors used by incoming passengers and peered through the glass at a small, slick plane parked at the gate.

"They're in there, huh?" Jim pushed on the door.

"No, Jim! Please wait." Gaye caught his arm.

"Wait for what, for God's sake?"

"Wait for the police, Jim. Please . . ."

"They won't let you in the plane. Come on upstairs and we'll talk to them on the radio. The lady's right. Call the police." Gaye was grateful for the man's support.

"The minute they see the police they'll take off. That pilot can't afford to be a part of a kidnapping, and Marla and her brothers can't afford the publicity. The old man would kill them."

"Then let's try and talk them into giving up."

"It makes sense, Jim," Gaye pleaded.

"All right, sweetheart. This is my wife, Tom. We were married today. It's a hell of a way to spend a wedding night."

"Congratulations, Jim. Best wishes, Mrs. Trumbull." He extended a hand to her, and Gaye put hers into it. "You're going to need all the help you can get to keep up with this fellow." He shot Jim a smiling glance. "How can an ugly old boy like you be so lucky."

Jim ignored his friend's attempt at light-heartedness and was already headed up the stairs. "We'll give it a try, but if they're not out of there in ten minutes, I'll turn the damn plane over!"

Tom opened the door to the glass-enclosed radio room. A man wearing a headset swiveled around on his chair.

"People are crazy. There's a damn fool coming in. I told him the airport was about to close down. He's coming in anyway."

"Where's he coming from?" Jim asked tersely.

"From the East. Hold on." He turned back to the radio, and Jim started for the door.

"Wait," Tom said. "Wait and talk. This guy will be in, in a few minutes, and then we'll radio the plane. They're not going to be able to stay out there all night. It's a blizzard, man."

"They could've sent for another plane. I'm not waiting."

Gaye and Tom followed Jim down the stairs again. At the double doors Tom said, "Wait until this plane lands and I'll help you roll out a boarding stair. Wait here, I'll be right back."

Jim paused. "All right. But I'm getting in that plane and getting my grandson if I have to take a crowbar and force open the door." He turned to Gaye and put his arm around her. "How are you doing, love?"

"I'm all right. I think we should call the police and let them handle it. You might get so mad you'll hurt someone, darling."

His arms tightened around her, and his lips smoothed the hair from her temple. "Don't worry. I won't do anything foolish, but they won't leave here with that boy, I promise you that!" She could feel the leashed anger and shuddered to think of that anger being directed at her. They stood quietly, holding on to each other, giving comfort by touching.

Tom returned. "The plane's down. As soon as they disembark and we get them out of the way, we'll go out."

Jim and Gaye turned to watch the plane turn slowly, pull into position guided by a man with a flashing amber light, and stop. The door was flung open almost immediately, and the stairway rolled down. Two people came down the stairway holding to the rail. The powerful gusts of snow-filled wind buffeted them.

Gaye turned her head away from them and buried her face against the smooth leather of Jim's coat. She was afraid for Jim, afraid for Johnny. If Jim tried to break into the plane they might shoot him! Oh, God! She couldn't bear it if anything happened to him. She clutched at his arms and felt him stiffen and draw away from her.

"What the hell!"

Gaye lifted her head, and her startled eyes saw a man in a black felt hat and an overcoat coming in through the double doors. Jim's hands seized her arms and lifted her away from him as if she were a small child. She saw Tom reach out and take hold of his arm, trying to restrain him.

"You're not going to have my grandson!" Jim shouted. "I'll fight to keep him and I'll fight dirty." The threatening words exploded from him in an angry torrent that carried into every corner of the building. He was shaking with rage.

Gaye took a step forward. "Mr. Lambert? Is that you?" she asked, bewilderment making her doubt her eyes.

"Yes, it's me, Mrs. Meiners. How are you?" The neat old gentleman carefully removed his hat and flicked the snow from it with his gloved hands.

"How the hell do you think she is?" Jim roared. "What's going on here? Do you know him?" he demanded roughly and grabbed Gaye's arm and spun her around.

"Yes! He came to the house with Mrs. Johnson. Jim . . . ?" Her pulse leaped with fear when she looked into his blazing eyes. "What is it? Do *you* know him?"

"You're damn right I know him!" he gritted through twisted lips. "He's my former father-in-law. The father of those damn fools who're trying to take MacDougle away from us. He's the kingpin of the family and just as rotten as the rest of them!"

"Oh, no!" Gaye sagged against him. She was sure she would faint. Her rubbery legs could scarcely hold her. What had she done? Why didn't she believe Jim when he cautioned her about strangers? The eyes she focused on the old gentleman standing calmly by were icy and accusing. "Mr. Lambert, why didn't you tell me who you were? You used me and you used Mrs. Johnson to get in the house. It was rotten of you!" The words came out through the lump of pain in her throat.

"Mr. Lambert-Moyer, you mean," Jim spit out caustically. "*The* Lambert-Moyer! Law! Stockmarket! Banking! Politics! And now, kidnapping!"

"Can we sit down and discuss this calmly?" Mr. Lambert spoke in a quiet voice. "You may find out that I'm not quite as rotten as you think."

"No, by God!" Jim shouted. "I'm going to get that boy!" Gaye could hear the anguish in his voice.

"Mr. Lambert, they've got Johnny out there." Gaye forced her tongue to make the necessary movements. "They came and took him while Jim and I were at the church. They didn't take his formula, and if they try to give him something else he'll be sick. Make them give him back!" Her eyes pleaded. "Please . . ."

"Don't beg, Gaye!" Jim's sharp command came from above her.

Gaye turned on him like a spitting kitten. "I'll beg, plead, get down on my knees and kiss his feet, if that's what it takes to get Johnny. Take your pride, Jim! Take your pride and shove it!" she shouted. She was so frightened and so steeped in misery she had to lash out at someone. She wasn't aware of the look of surprise that came over Jim's face or the way his nostrils flared with pride when he recognized her fighting spirit.

"She doesn't have to beg, Jim. I came out here a few weeks ago to find out what sort of person was in charge of my great-grandson. I visited in her home and returned when she wasn't expecting me. I came away well satisfied that she was far more capable of shaping a young life than Marla and Crissy. I told Marla and my sons to back off and be satisfied that the boy has a good home. I found out this morning what they're up to. I apologize for the grief they've caused you, Mrs. Meiners."

"Jim and I were married this morning, Mr. Lambert. Our hearts are full of love for Johnny." Gaye broke away from Jim. "Can you make them give him back to us? At least let us take care of him until all this is decided."

"It's decided, Gaye," Jim exclaimed angrily.

Gaye ignored him and spoke directly to Mr. Lambert. "They're out there in the plane waiting for permission to take off. If they take him out of the country we'll never see him again." The words came with a sob. "Jim's going out there. Someone will be hurt. . . ."

"There's no need for Jim to do anything. They know that I'm here. They heard my pilot talking to the tower and knew I was coming in. I've instructed my pilot to tell them that I'm coming aboard." Mr. Lambert's voice was low-pitched and even-tenored, as if nothing could move him to anger.

"Let me go with you. What will they do? Will they let you have Johnny?" Gaye struggled to keep from crying.

"They'll let me have him. I still control the family purse strings; therefore, I still control the family." He said it rather sadly. "Try to keep this . . . wild man calm until I get back." He glanced at Jim and then set his hat carefully on his head.

Gaye watched him go back out into the blizzard. In the wavering light from the terminal she saw the man who'd come with him take his arm as they braced themselves against the wind. She watched until they went up the hastily rolled-out boarding stair, then turned back hopefully to Jim.

"Oh, darling! It's going to be all right. I can't believe that Mr. Lambert is Johnny's great-grandfather."

"Well, he is. I always rather liked the old boy, even if he did do a lousy job raising his kids." Jim put his arm around her and pulled her close to him. "He's always stood by them even when they were wrong, and I'll be surprised if he doesn't this time. We'll wait and see. Something had better happen soon. I'm about at the end of my tether."

They stood with their faces pressed to the glass doors, straining to see through the blowing snow. Gaye held tightly to Jim's hand. The minutes seemed like hours.

"He was nice, Jim. I liked him. He sat at the kitchen table and ate sugar cookies while I fed Johnny. We talked about . . . different things. I even gave him the recipe for my mother's sugar cookies." She talked to keep from thinking about what was going on in the plane.

"You what?" Jim asked in a brittle tone of surprise.

"He wanted my sugar-cookie recipe. They *are* good, Jim. You've downed an entire batch all by yourself. I copied it off for him. He was going to make them, he said. I can't help it if he's Marla's father. I like him." She chattered nervously, completely unaware that her nails were digging into Jim's hand.

"Evidently he likes you," Jim said slowly, and his warm breath made a mist on the cold glass of the door. "I can't fault him for that."

When the plane door opened, Gaye heard Jim suck air deeply into his lungs. She squeezed his hand and kept her eyes riveted on the door. Oh, God! she prayed. Let it be all right. This man I love has such strong feelings, is so . . . violent when he hates! But when he loves, he loves —

One shadowy figure came down the steps first, helping the one that followed. They reached the snow-packed concrete of the runway, and Gaye could see that Mr. Lambert was carrying a bundle. Her breath stopped and held, then let out in a gush when the door opened and she heard Johnny's angry muffled cries. She rushed forward, her eyes brimming with tears.

The elderly man lifted the blanket from the baby's red, tear-wet face and placed him in her arms. Jim was beside her. She was conscious of the relief in his big body as his arms enfolded them and he hugged her and the infant to him.

"Thank you, Mr. Lambert. Oh, thank you . . ." she whispered tearfully. Then, "Jim . . . get his bottle — he's so hungry!"

"Is he all right?"

"Yes, yes. Sshhh . . . darling," she crooned. "It's all right. We've got you now. . . . Sshhh . . . you'll have your bottle and then we'll go home. Hurry, Jim —"

Jim's fingers were shaking, but he managed to get the nipple on the bottle turned in the right direction and in the baby's mouth. The cries ceased immediately, and there was only an occasional sob as Johnny sucked vigorously on the nipple. Jim led Gaye to a chair. He knelt down beside them and held the bottle while she peeled back the blankets.

"He's so wet!" she whispered to Jim. "We've got to change him before we take him home."

"Let him eat first," he whispered back. "Then I'll hold him while you change him. I'll get Tom to follow us in his four-wheel drive. I'm afraid the roads will be closed soon."

Gaye's eyes were wet and shining. Johnny's small hand curved contentedly about her finger. She blinked rapidly to hold back the tears.

"Oh, Jim. I couldn't bear to lose him." She leaned over the baby and rested her forehead against Jim's cheek.

When Jim stood he towered over Mr. Lambert-Moyer. He extended his hand. "Thank you, sir."

"You won't have any more trouble, Jim. I'll see to it." The old gentleman's eyes kept returning to Gaye and the baby. "You may have got a lemon the first time, Jim. But you hit the jackpot the second time around. I hope you appreciate her."

"I do. Believe me, I do. She's a good mother for our grandson." His throat clogged and he cleared it noisily.

"Mr. Lambert . . ." Gaye held up her free

hand to grasp his. "Please keep in touch. You'll always be welcome in our home. Come and see us. Johnny should know his great-grandfather."

"I'd like that." Mr. Lambert gripped her hand tightly. "He may like my sugar cookies even better than yours." Gaye noticed he was blinking his eyes rather rapidly.

"Did you really make them?" she asked lightly.

"Of course. I find they brown on the bottom much better if you use a stainless-steel cookie sheet."

"Really? I'll have to get one. Good-bye, Mr. Lambert. I'll never be able to thank you enough."

"Good-bye, Mrs. Trumbull. And thanks are not necessary. It was my duty to do the best I could for my great-grandson. Good-bye, John," he said softly and touched the baby's cheek briefly with his fingertips, then extended his hand to Jim. "Good-bye, Jim."

They watched him until he reached the door, where he paused and set his black felt hat carefully on his head before he went out into the blizzard.

Jim, wearing only his pajama bottoms, lay sprawled on the couch in front of the fireplace. His head rested on the arm at one end, his bare feet on the other. A plate with a half-eaten piece of wedding cake was on the floor beside the couch. The rest of the cake sat on the dining room table, with several pink sugar roses missing and deep grooves where small fingers had scooped up icing. An apologetic note from Lila lay beside it.

Gaye came down the stairs, spotted the dish on the floor and came to pick it up. Jim grabbed her arm, causing her to lose her balance. She came crashing down on top of him. She heard a whoosh as the air exploded from his lungs when she landed on his stomach.

"Ha! Serves you right for being so rough. All you had to do was ask me."

"Ask you what?"

"Well . . . you know. To come and lie down on top of you so you can . . ."

"Can what?"

"Put your hands up under my night-gown?" she whispered and stretched out full-length on him.

"And?"

"You're impossible! Did you call to see if your mother and your aunt were all right?"

"Of course I did. Don't change the subject. What did you think I wanted to do to you?"

"I don't know," she said innocently and worked her palm between his hard-muscled stomach and her soft one. "The same thing you did to me as soon as we got Johnny to bed? Is this what we're talking about?" She felt his body jolt from her touch and laughed against his cheek.

His hands slid under her nightgown and cupped her bare buttocks, holding her tightly against him, capturing her hand between them.

"Are you about at the end of your tether, love?" she whispered teasingly. "You were marvelously patient while I was getting Johnny settled."

"*MacDougle* is going to have to learn to share!"

"*Johnny* is just a baby. He's too young to learn anything."

"*MacDougle* is old enough to know all he has to do is cry and you come running."

"That's because he's been through a traumatic experience, as we have."

"When we get our baker's dozen am I going to get just one-thirteenth of your time?"

"Thirteen? That means I'll be pregnant for almost ten years!"

"You'll be cute pregnant."

"I'll be fat! I'll have to go to the exercise

class three times a week."

"Oh, no! I'll give you all the exercise you need." He moved her rhythmically against the part of him that had sprung to rigid hardness. "It'll be a lot more fun," he whispered against her mouth.

She placed her lips firmly against his and kissed him deeply, thrilled that he responded, yet let her have her way with him. She felt a warm desire burn from deep within and spread through her. She answered the gentle thrusts of his hips with a pressure of her own. Her clinging lips lifted a fraction from his, her forehead rested against him, their eyelashes tangled.

"I love you, my caveman, my gentle giant." She filled her two hands with his wild dark hair.

"I love you, too."

She had never hoped to see such love in a man's eyes when they looked at her. She felt truly loved and cherished.

"I like to feel the weight of you on me." He slid his palms over her buttocks and thighs.

"Is that what makes your heart pound?"

"Is that my heart? I thought it was yours."

"How about throwing me over your shoulder and carrying me off to your cave?" she asked in a seductive whisper.

"Arrrr . . . aw!" He snapped his teeth together. His reaction was so quick it almost startled her. He rolled, got to his feet with her in his arms, flung her over his shoulder, gave her bottom a swat and took the stairs two at a time.

The employees of Thorndike Press hope you have enjoyed this Large Print book. All our Thorndike and Wheeler Large Print titles are designed for easy reading, and all our books are made to last. Other Thorndike Press Large Print books are available at your library, through selected bookstores, or directly from us.

For information about titles, please call:
(800) 223-1244

or visit our Web site at:
www.gale.com/thorndike
www.gale.com/wheeler

To share your comments, please write:
Publisher
Thorndike Press
295 Kennedy Memorial Drive
Waterville, ME 04901